Parables
for
Living
v.3

by
Rev. Daniel Kerr

TOPICS

<u>INTRODUCTION</u>

Our lives are complicated. Our lives are busy with just living day to day. When we can take the time to read what the Gospels have in store for us then, through time, our days become more blessed. Each of the Gospels that the parables are based on is a message to each of you to live your lives fuller and with more grace and mercy. I know, that when I read the Gospels it gives me insight to the things that pop up in my busy life. It's strange that way. The words of God speak differently to each of us because we all come at this God and Jesus belief from a different vantage point. That's OK because the words of God will speak to you wherever you are.

I invite you to read the Gospels in each subject and then the parable and the words that go with it. I hope and pray that they will enlighten your lives and fill them with the love that can only come from our Father.

This book and all subsequent editions is dedicated to my wife, Jane, who has stood by me when the times were uncertain. It's really her faith that has prodded and pushed me thus far. She has shown great patience throughout the years and, without her by my side, I have no clue where I would be. My love to her, always and forever.

<u>BELIEF</u>

Fulfillment at Hand

Gospel – Mark 1:9 – 15
References – Joel 2:30 – 31

There once was an old man who spent his life saving and scrimping for his golden years. He was so adamant about this that he passed opportunities to experience many of the adventures that he was invited to when he was younger. He never married as that would take his focus off of saving and put it on other people.

As he grew older, his savings grew but the people around him lessened. Many of his friends died off and, pretty soon, this old man was left with no one but himself. On his deathbed, he lamented that his focus on his later years eliminated his focus on his present life. Few came to his funeral as many that he grew up with had already passed on and he never made friends with any new people younger than he.

It was said that it was a shame that this old man had never shared his life experiences with anyone as his own history had to be filled with many events because he had lived almost all of the 20th century.

When his lonely time was fulfilled, his preparation was not in what counted, the living people here and his heavenly life, but in that which held no real longevity, his lonely earthly life.

As we reflect on this old man, we can sometimes see ourselves striving for earthly comfort while ignoring heavenly preparation.

****

God's timing is everything. We don't know what's gonna happen tomorrow but we can be sure that our Father does. We don't know what lays in store for us tomorrow but we can be sure that our Father does. We don't even know what our kids and grandkids will have to face in the coming days, months and years but we can be sure that our Father does.

This is a time where we're to reflect not only on the finished, what has happened in our past, but make preparations for the future. A future that many sitting here and watching online have deep reservations about. Some may have a temporary joy but our expectations of our earthly leaders almost always comes up short.

They, like us, always fall short when it comes to the expectations of our Father. Expectations that are spelled out in the list of ten revelations that He gave to Moses on the mountain and that Jesus came and condensed down to two.

And because none of us can possibly fulfill any part of that original ten or the condensed two we need the forgiveness of Jesus and the absolution of our failings and then we're back to the reservation part.

The part that keeps us looking up to the cross for that assurance that we really do have hope. Hope and belief that our change can be something that holds us for eternity.

Noah illustrates to us just what that change can mean. God destroyed the earth and virtually everything in it, with the exception of Noah and his family, because He was distraught over the very evils everyone was doing. Nothing was too low. They had broken everything that God put in front of them.

They thought themselves to be Gods. And they incurred the wrath of the one true God in the process. God said enough is enough. And so God flooded the earth and everyone who thought they had all the answers found out that they really didn't. They weren't kings of their domains after all.

And then there's Ezekiel. A returning of the chosen people of God back to the land they once occupied. That has already happened in the 1960s. There was no Palestine in ancient history. That territory was original to Samaria, Judea and Galilee among other civilizations. In fact, in no place in the Old nor the New Testaments does the word Palestine appear. Not in the Hebrew or the Greek.

The term was used to describe a type of people. Not a nationality. The "Palestinian" people in Israel's homeland today are refugees from all the other surrounding Arab states in the area. They are people caste out, or thrown off, from their true homelands. Palestine, as it's referred to today, did not exist in the beginning. It does not exist now. It never has existed. It will never exist because God already gave that land to the Jews.

But Jesus makes a startling statement, "The time is fulfilled, and the kingdom of God is at hand." Much of this meaning underneath is prophetic in nature. Some of it is the present where we're to prepare our hearts and our minds for whatever is to happen tomorrow.

One second, or one minute, to God is like a thousand years to us. That can also apply to our tomorrows. Jesus tells us to be prepared. To be watchful. Elijah has already come back once in the form of John the Baptist. He'll come again to tell us too.

The end of days, the time of fulfillment started when Jesus came back from Hell. When He went down there and cleared it out. Claimed it back showing Satan that He was in charge. That Satan had no more true dominion.

The parable illustrates what can happen to us all when our focus is on a tomorrow that may never happen and, if it does, the mindset that God is not in charge, I am, is what keeps us from enjoying and participating in the lives of those around us.

The old man in the parable tells us to concentrate on the people and times around you because all will soon be gone and then you are left with literally nothing and your legacy will be zero. What we're remembered for is what we leave behind not what has not happened in the future.

<u>BELIEF</u>

Gather the Lost

Gospel – John 6:1 – 21

References – Deuteronomy 7:1; 2nd Kings 4

There once was a woodworker who spent his days creating designs that were most unusual. This woodworker would gather all his tools. Gather all the wood he was gonna need from prior projects. Gather all the nails and glue and clamps that his lifetime of assembling projects taught him he was gonna need and then he just sat there.

Sometimes he would get up in the mornings, go out into his shop and just sit there. He didn't know when he would start a new project because he had to wait. Wait for some idea or inspiration to hit him before he could start. Some of his friends would pass by and many would see him just sitting there. Sitting there in contemplation.

Then, out of the blue, this guy would begin. He wouldn't stop until what he wanted to create had been completed. Barely ate even. And the end result? It was always amazing to look upon by those that were invited to see it when he was finished.

You see, this woodworker knew that the true knowledge of all that he would need came out of his time in thought. He was looking for that inspiration given to him by something or someone else to spur him on. He was looking to create something that would feed the senses of all those that bought his works.

And he was looking for the words to give him the instructions to carry out the tasks that would allow others to get a feel for the heavenly design that he perceived. He took bits and pieces of what was left over and assembled them to a complete project just like Jesus did with the leftovers from the feeding of the many people.

****

In our Gospel we have two miracles, one is the feeding of the five thousand men. Some put that estimate at between 9 and 15 thousand people in all. The second is Jesus walking on water. Each of the three Gospels, Mark, Matthew and John, have a different take on the walking.

Each of these accounts is different in some ways but the one thing that's the same in each of them is the count of what was left after the crowds had their fill. Twelve baskets. Twelve left overs after everyone had been satisfied. Twelve apostles filling the twelve baskets with many broken parts.

The feeding miracle always goes hand in hand with Jesus walking on water. Very rarely in all four Gospels is there a complete agreement on events. Usually, there are some variations but this gathering of the loaves and fishes by the apostles is almost identical. The use of bread harkens to Exodus where God's feeding the people with manna, a sort of bread.

Twelve left overs of what was once used but has now been gathered up. Sort of like the twelve apostles and the people themselves. Once they were ordinary people but, after their times with the crowds, after going out into the countryside to spread the good news, after ministering to the many, when they had come back together, had gathered together, there were twelve.

But, this is really meant for you and me. It wasn't whole loaves of bread and fish that were brought back to Jesus. It wasn't pieces reassembled like they were new. It was broken pieces. Broken like you and me. Gathered up and given over to Jesus to place in the safety of that basket.

Wanting to mend our broken lives and give our lives over to the apostles so that they could then, so that you could then, go back out into the countryside and tell the story. Tell your story. Lead others, gather together others, for this feast also.

The numbers of baskets left over references back to the Old Testament. The number twelve almost always refers to the twelve tribes of Israel and it just happens to be the national number of the People of God. It was this establishing of the original tribe of twelve by God after the Exodus.

So, the mention of the twelve baskets of leftovers is neither a coincidence nor accident as Jesus' actions are neither either but His actions are a continual reference to prophesy and Old Testament numbers.

While we can rest in the knowledge that we're in God's family, we must keep in mind that even the disciples, themselves, needed help. They didn't come up with the loaves and fishes on their own. A little boy brought them to them.

Sometimes we wait for others to make a move before we're willing to put our foot forward and what results is that those who have been doing the lifting, like the little boy in this Gospel sort of wear out. We're called to work together so that the whole of the body of Christ is lived out.

The parable illustrates that it is the bits and pieces that we have that complete us and those around us. That can fill others with an awe that can only come from the direction and inspiration of God and Jesus. The woodworker drew his vision from the ideas that came to him after sitting quietly and pondering what was needed from him to enlighten others.

We can do the same in that many times our world is so busy with the day to day that we cannot see where we can use the leftovers from our own lives to fill the hunger in others. The parable tells of how the woodworker uses what was left from previous projects to make completely new ones. That is how we are to do too thereby helping to complete the lives of those around us so they can see new beauty in the ordinary.

<u>BELIEF</u>

Reject or Neglect

Gospel – John 6:56 – 71

References – John 1:1 – 5

There once was a girl who bought a pearl necklace at a flea market and was convinced that it was an heirloom once belonging to a queen. She saw a similar one in a history book and fell in love with it and when she ran across the one that looked like it, she just fell in love with it and had to have it. But it was very expensive even for flea market value and the price of other things for sale.

When the store owner was asked why this necklace was so expensive, the store owner told her that it was a necklace that had been handed down from generation to generation and was always thought to have come from royalty. This convinced the girl that she was right so she spent every last dime she had to obtain it.

When she got home, she made plans. She decided she needed to have it appraised and when she did the appraiser told her that while it was very old there was no way to confirm the authenticity of it.

So the girl went to another appraiser who told her the same thing. So the girl went to another with the same results. This went on some time and the girl was beginning to have doubts except that something about it kept nagging her on.

She finally wore it to a fancy dinner. It was there that decedents of the queen were in appearance and as the people lined up to greet the royal family, the girl stood among them. When the royal family greeted her, they could not take their eyes off the necklace she wore.

Afterwards, an assistant to the family approached the girl and offered to buy the necklace from her. The girl told them that she had thought it belonged to a queen of years back but the assistant told her no it did not but was owned by the queen's daughter who had lost it after a terrible accident. The royal family has been distraught over the accident ever since, not because of the necklace but because the accident claimed the life of the daughter. The girl, compassionate for the family, took the necklace off and gave it to the assistant.

You see, regardless of what we may believe, sometimes what we believe may be altered by what the real truth is but the end result will always hit home in our hearts if we can accept it rather than reject it.

****

I'm frequently asked and I constantly debate with others the age-old question of "Why do bad things happen to good people if there's an all loving God?" One could even ask if there's a just God then why do good things happen to bad people?

But I believe that it's more rational to accept the faith that one has been given to believe in a God that lets us be human than to discount and reject that same faith by saying that there must not be a God in the first place.

This chapter, in John, is broken up simply because the whole of this chapter would take too long to go through on only one Sunday. From how God uses what we have to multiply for us, which allows us to see all that He has created and shared with us, to Jesus showing us that He's the one that feeds us, rather than Moses, in the desert, to warning us that it's so easy to distort our view of this world with the influences of those around us, to destroying the concept that anyone, anywhere, at any time, must have a come to Jesus moment to be accepted by the one that has already come to you.

So, in the reality that is our here and now, how does this help us or even give us the strength we need? It's thru this life that's Jesus the Christ that we can see the little reminders set around us every day and, in those times of trouble or heartbreak or fear, it's those reminders that we have not been forsaken.

The Gospel of John is about relationship. Your relationship with God, Jesus and each other as the ecclesia. It's about a relationship that God has created and instilled in each of us regardless of our ability to define or understand it, it's still in existence and nothing you nor I can do will eliminate it because we didn't create it in the first place.

The relationship that God and Christ has established is beyond our ability to comprehend simply because it's vast and we're not. It's because of this relationship that agnostics are frustrated because they're not able to humanly define it.

But it's because of this vast relationship that is unimaginable that gives the believer the confidence to proclaim that God and Christ are real.

The parable illustrates that most of us have an idea of what Jesus and God are like but when we're face with the reality of who they are, they truth becomes greater than what we had originally hoped for.

What we may hope for, in this life, can never be compared to what is waiting for us in the next. We can reject the notion of an afterlife. We can neglect the comforting words of Jesus that calls out to us. But to do so, robs us of the possibilities that the truth is real.

<u>BELIEF</u>

What do You Really Want to Know?

Gospel – Matthew 21:23 – 32

References – Matthew 7:29; Romans 10:19

There once was a young man who lived with his mother. Now, his mother suffered from severe depression so much so that the young man wouldn't allow her to view anything that was negative or just generally bad news.

He would wake up every morning and begin to cut out all the stories from the local newspaper that had bad news in it. He would make sure that all the bills were kept out of her sight. And he would change the channel on the radio broadcasts so that she couldn't hear any of the things going on in the world that would be negative news.

He did this for many years and his main concern was that she lived her life in a manner that only good and positive things were in her presence. The only problems were that there were many bill collectors phoning them since he couldn't work, the absence of news about the community in their hometown paper deprived her of knowing what was happening to her friends, and the nation was at war.

This led to both of them being evicted from their home for non-payment with no one to assist, left them with no friends to turn to and, to make matters worse, the young man was drafted to go fight in the war which left the mother with absolutely no one to lean on.

Completely alone and unprepared. Blind even though she saw. Deaf even though she heard. Dumb even though she had all her faculties.

****

Expectations. You know, this passage speaks about expectations not always being our realities in the here and now. The chief priests sat in judgment of Jesus in the prior chapters because they've put out of their conscious all thoughts of self-examination or self-incrimination. If not that then they certainly tried convincing themselves that they weren't the hypocrites that they portended to be against.

But the choices they had to make because of their silence told more to those listening, the crowd, than if they had said anything. Of course, we can find ourselves doing what these leaders have done. We can make snap decisions and then learn, later on, that what we decided was the best course of action, upon further review, was probably not the course we should've taken.

Now, Jesus was pinning the elders and Pharisees down with their response, or lack thereof, to their persecution of John the Baptist and by caveat, Jesus, Himself. If they acknowledged the authority of John then they would display, to the crowd, their hypocrisy. If they remained silent, then they are like the second group that Jesus has laid out here and condemned by their own laws. By fiat, Jesus is telling them to make that choice about Him too.

Jesus is recognized with these authorities by the crowds who have heard Him, seen Him, and were healed by Him. This isn't something the elders and the High Priests could ignore because in order to do that they lose their standing among their people and are no longer the rulers they've come to believe about themselves.

Maybe a real question for all of us is do we arrange our own lives and our associates so that our lives become the lie of convenience or an imitation of those leaders of Jesus' day? I think, if we look and examine ourselves closely, many times we do.

I read and hear and communicate with people who aren't concerned with the real truth because they view the truth as somehow evolving and self-directed. They view people from their skin tone alone and categorize everyone based on that surface observation.

They march in the streets because their sense of justice is somehow more valid than the history that is absolute and their view of that history is skewed because some famous person or organization with a catchy slogan or hash tag told them all are to blame except those who are supposedly oppressed.

This passage contradicts all that you see going on in our streets and by some of our ruling class. This passage says that when we encounter another brother or sister and they walk away, then we're to pursue them just like the first son rather than the second.

Folks, not knowing what to do or say is not really the problem. Not wanting to know what to do or say is the real problem because it might upset your own understanding or expectations of the outcome. When the search stops, life ceases to exist. But, a complete and full knowledge of God's word can never be fully understood because it covers such a vast expanse of knowledge but that understanding must still be pursued.

The parable illustrates that what we want to know is less than what we need to know and what we observe, if not taken with the truth that is in it, cannot help us to know anything more than what we don't want to know.

The son was hampering his mother. By keeping all the bad news from her, he wasn't allowing her to understand the truth that was all around them and she suffered because of it. Jesus told the chief priests the same thing. What they saw they couldn't grasp because it would lessen their own sense of power and righteousness so they remained outside the grace of the Father.

BELIEF

Where Is The Party?

Gospel – Matthew 22:1 – 14
References – Isaiah 5:24; John 6:60 – 70

One day a man got an invitation to a big fund raiser put on by one of the candidates who were running for office in his town. Now, this man was not necessarily a huge fan of the candidate but he decided to go anyways just to hear what that person thought about what was going on in the town.

When he arrived, he found lots of banners and bumper stickers and signs but he also noticed that there weren't very many people there. The few that were there only talked about how bad the opponent was and nothing about what the candidate stood for or would do or how the candidate could actually get it done. The specifics.

Then, when the candidate got up to speak, he also only spoke about how bad it was in the town and how he would change it for the better but he also didn't mention any specific ways in how that would actually get done. What it would cost. Who would benefit and who would suffer. Those that were already in attendance cheered and clapped but they never questioned the candidate in the specifics either.

When this man had his opportunity to have a face to face with the candidate, he was told that he would have to get back to him or that it was on the literature or only that the other guy was so bad or even how could he even question the candidates credentials.

Those that were crowded around this man also chimed in on the same note. Scorning the man for his descent. So, the man was booted out of the event.

****

The Gospel parable is a juxtaposition on the Gospel in that the point of Jesus' parable is that there'll be many that come to the party but not so many that'll decide to wear the full clothes of Christ.

There'll be many at the party who like to talk the talk but many that just can't seem to walk the walk because their true values are rooted in a history that's false. Rooted in half-truths and clouded over with misinformation that they don't want to see because it would then question everything about their own sense of worth.

There'll be many that gather around those that are new to this whole belief thing but many of those that surround them will react much like those at the fundraiser. Expecting full compliance without giving much of anything as to the substance of what this whole Jesus thing is.

There'll be those that reject the newcomers, or even the old timers depending on their views, so that those people never have the chance to get answers to the questions as to why all of this matters in the first place.

You see, we can be like the crowd and just congregate together, which is really great and all, and, in the process, cause others who just don't get it to never come back because there ain't no meat on the table. No meat to what the true message is.

Nothing anyone can sink their teeth into because we tell em if they'll just read their bibles more or just hand them a pamphlet or two or even give them a bible without answering any of the abiding questions that's in their hearts about what all this means to them, they'll exit without any contribution just like the man did in our parable.

This original dinner party is the Messianic banquet given by God, the king, for all those of His creation. This is God's fundraiser. Where everyday people come and give of themselves, not to God's reelection or anything but give of themselves to all those in their communities. God's reaffirmation that He's the one in charge.

Folks, the fact of the matter is that we cannot presume grace. We can rest ourselves upon it. Know that we can have it. Receive it when it's offered. But we cannot assume we'll automatically get it just because we're walking and talking and breathing.

However, the Jews did just that and the end result was the total destruction of Jerusalem back in 70 C.E. You see, they were the first guests.

Having questions of what does all this mean is a good way to begin. The early disciples did that too but many of them turned their backs even after seeing for themselves all the miracles that Jesus did. They were the second group.

But to keep from being the guy that got thrown out in our parable requires acceptance of the person you were designed to be. A disciple. A disciple of Christ. A person that hears what your neighbor says, listens with intent, and then walks that person down their own path to the light that you've been shown in whatever manner that may be.

We are those folks that God sent out His slaves to gather up and bring to sit at the table. The table of the Father. To the party. We're the folks that come into God's house with our brokenness and seek His forgiveness.

The parable illustrates our own congregations. The people in the church. The ones that are already here and the ones that are looking for a place that can give them reassurance and peace. A place that's inviting and, also, has a message that has some meat on it. Something they can chew on the following days and, hopefully, ponder on what it really means.

BLESSINGS

Where Do We Fit In?

Gospel – John 1:1 – 18

References – Jeremiah 1:5; Ephesians 1:4; Hebrews 1:1 – 2

There once were two families who lived right next door to each other. One of the families had twelve kids while the other only had one.

The family with twelve kids always seemed to struggle to survive while the family with one seemed to have it all. The family with twelve kids always seemed to have toys and other household things strewn about the yard while the family with one didn't seem to have anything out in which the neighbors could see. The family with twelve kids always seemed to be in turmoil while the family with one always seemed to be at peace. The family with twelve kids was very public in the neighborhood while the family with one was very private.

But what the neighbors didn't know was that the family of twelve was always helping the family with one because that single child, the one child, had a disease that kept him from going outside, interacting with others outside of his bubble, playing with ordinary toys unless they had been sterilized.

The family with twelve was always so busy trying to bring a sense of joy to that one, lone boy, that they really didn't have any opportunity to focus on the orderings of their own home since they were so engaged in the social life of the one that had no society outside of the restrictions of his own little world.

Unfortunately, the family of the single child didn't publicize their child's affliction because they didn't want the publicity. The family, with twelve, found out by accident and they decided that it was their mission and God given duty to bring a sense of normalcy to an otherwise abnormal situation.

****

John sets the stage for the overall explanation of the origins and the mission of Jesus before this world was created and, later, here on this earth.

John tries to put this whole God and Jesus and us thing into perspective and his way of telling it is to reinforce the notion and belief that Jesus arrived in this world specifically to get ordinary people to finally listen to what God meant for them going all the way back to the Sinai where they wandered around for 40 years. And yet, they still missed the boat.

The Jewish remnants couldn't seem to look past the physical into the spiritual. We know this to be a fact because of all the rules and regulations they created which caused those original 10 commandments to just explode.

John took Jesus and made three separate truths that apply to you and me as well as the folks that were reading his stuff back then.

John uses the word, "world". It's "kosmos" in the Greek and it references specifically to humanity and its domain – not creation. In other words, it references us. You and me. John's saying through the words, "He was in the world" which could really be restated as, "He was in humanity."

The second part, "And the world was made through Him" could also be restated as "And humanity was made through Him."

Folks, that falls in line with us being created in the image of God, Himself. Because Jesus was begotten from the Father, when the beginning was just starting as well as nine months before Christmas Day, we too have been begotten of the Father from time immemorial. From the beginning.

Which leads me into the third part of this, "And the world did not know Him" which can be restated as, "And humanity did not know Him." If John is correct, and I'm pretty sure he is, we, here, really have our eyes and our ears closed to the real saviorific extent of the one that came to us in the stall of that manger.

The humanity of us all is that we only see, most of the time, what we want to see. Not what's really there. We all have doubts especially during our difficult times. Surface doubts as to knowing that God and Jesus are active in our lives. When things are upended in our lives, we tend to look around and wonder what's the real meaning of all of this.

You know, God is listening. Sometimes it may not appear so but He's listening never the less. Sometimes it's in ways that we can't tell immediately but many times reflect, on looking back, and see His hand in all that happened.

Jesus came here to us to show us that there really is another way. Not with the work your way into heaven sort of thing but with the your accepting your way to heaven way. Jesus came down here to show us that even one who has the ultimate power to stop evil allows it to continue because without that choice between good or bad, you and me, we just become robots and there ain't no love in that.

The parable illustrates that even those that everyone thinks is challenged can see a need in other families or people that are desperate for the kind of love and help that can be found. Our society puts people into categories by default. But it's the individuals within that category that have the choice and the chance to still break out by going outside of themselves. That's what the family does in this parable.

<u>BLESSINGS</u>

Who Do We Become?

Gospel – John 1:1 – 9, 19 – 28

References – Genesis 1:1; 2nd Kings 2:11; Isaiah 40

There once lived a hermit, high in hills, above a small town. The inhabitants of this small town told stories about this hermit but the origins of those stories had long been lost to who authored them. So, with each passing year, the stories grew bigger and bigger.

One such story had the hermit as a warrior who fought off invaders from the past. Others had him as a broken hearted man who was jilted at the altar. One even had him as a man whose family had all perished in a famine of years past. But no one knew, for sure, what the truth was about this loner. Some didn't even know, as a matter of fact, if the hermit was even still up there, they all just assumed so. These stories went on for years and years and grew each time they were retold.

But, one day, the old hermit appeared in town. He had to see the doctor because he had tripped and broken his ankle.

All the townsfolk gathered around as each wanted to know the truth of this man. And the doctor asked him why he had secluded himself high on that hill all these years. The hermit told the doctor that he had not secluded himself but that the townspeople had originally refused to come to him.

He had built a wonderful vacation spot with fantastic views and glorious gardens. It was his intention that this would be a wonderful get away for those people laboring down below at no cost to them. Many years ago, he spread word that he had completed this veritable Eden and was ready to receive visitors.

But no one came. No one bothered. No one believed. So they made up stories about him and he quit asking for them.

****

The whole point of John's Gospel is based upon these words, "In the beginning was the Word, and the Word was with God, and the Word was God." John mimics Genesis 1 verse 1 but says it in a humanistic way.

In his view, and mine, what this verse says is that even before there was such a thing as time, a measurement that we've determined to be valid, there is, not was, is God. And through

God, the Holy Spirit, or the Word, the pneuma, and through that, Jesus the Christ.

The Word becoming flesh is the decisive event in all of human history because it changes the dynamic of the relationship between God, the Father, and us. It changes it because God created something, Jesus, through the Holy Spirit to be mixed within our own DNA to bring us closer to Him in order that we may be able to spend our eternity with Him, blameless.

Sometimes we become lost in all of this. Sometimes we know, in our hearts, that what's said, right here in Scripture, is the truth but the many events of our daily lives brings questions and doubts.

Jesus existed way before He was born of Mary but God used the purity of Mary to carry on His master plan of our salvation because it's only through the descendancy of Mary that Jesus would be able to be born pure. Jesus became of the line of David through adoption. Adoption by Joseph.

And we're also forever adopted by Jesus through our own baptism. Adopted through our belief in the faith that God has already instilled in each of us as part of the framework of our very own DNA core.

But our acceptance of Jesus as the one and only Savior and our own baptisms clean our lines going forward. Our acceptance of our Savior purifies our lives and our future generations. We speak this when we reaffirm the baptism of others.

Folks, John tells the story of Jesus in just 5 verses. Five simple phrases that speak volumes to what is to come next. Through the life of Jesus, what He reveals about God is what He reveals about Himself.

It should cause us to ask ourselves what do we reveal about our own selves every time we look in the mirror or when we encounter someone on the street. It might cause us to ask ourselves do we reveal the heart of a disciple or the heart made from the earth.

But, like the townsfolks in our parable, the people in power would much rather make the truth about Jesus what they want it to be rather than what it is. It's as if they have discounted the promises of the kingdom just like the people did about the hermit's place.

The parable illustrates that we can become what is said about us if we cannot hold onto the promises of Jesus. The hermit was not always the way he was but the people preferred to hold onto the myths that they wrote themselves and the hermit allowed that lie to take hold and blossom. We can do the same. It all depends on what our mission in our lives is about and how we go about executing that mission.

EXPECTATIONS

Listening

Gospel – Mark 6:1 – 13

References – Numbers 35:30; Deuteronomy 19:15;

Nehemiah 5:13

There once was a family that had two young boys. These were your normal, rambunctious boys who would get into all kinds of trouble. Nothing serious but their actions had to be addressed by their parents on a weekly basis. The parents were at their wits end but they just figured the boys would grow out of it. As most little boys do when they grow up.

But the boys didn't and it seemed that the older they got the more serious the trouble. Soon enough, the now young men proceeded to show, to all around them, their total ignorance of the generally acceptable rules of society so the parents decided that they be sent to a camp for those that were headed in the wrong directions for their lives.

Once at the camp, the intake officer read over the rules and punishment for the breaking of those rules. He looked at the two boys. One had his head down and the other was grinning from ear to ear in defiance. But it seemed strange to the officer so he decided to have both of them tested. The one with his head down was diagnosed as deaf and the other a social misfit.

So the instructor took the one who was deaf and fitted him with tools to help him understand. The other, the instructor assigned the severest hard work.

When the hearing boy complained why he had to do the hard work while his brother didn't, the instructor told him that his deaf brother didn't have to because he never heard the rules to living a life as a contribution to society.

The misfit had to do the work because he did hear those rules and decided that he didn't have to obey. In addition, the misfit knew of his brother's condition and did nothing to help.

****

Many, if not most, people have a tendency to hold on to preconceived ideas of how the world works and the things around them. They were guilty of this in Jesus' day and we have certainly not changed in the 2,000 plus years since.

The Gospel comes down to the folks in Jesus' own home town not being able to both see nor hear the one true God that was standing right there before them. And missing the true message that Jesus was there to give. Automatically discounting Him for who he was during a previous time and substituting their own memories of Him as a child.

Jesus was the proverbial gorilla walking and talking among the people that were so focused on their own lives and the mundane expectations of the history and traditions of their day that they missed the true message and person of God. Jesus was the proverbial gorilla in the room that had come home. Those in His home town just couldn't see the man before them nor could they grasp the Savior underneath.

I believe that Jesus was in a no-win situation. Society, in those days, was much more different than today. Those who watched Him grow up would seem to forever view him as just another carpenter.

What Jesus is saying to His disciples is to go. Take with you a brother so that the words that you speak and the miracles you perform are attested by each other. Jesus says go and make disciples of all nations that each and every one has the opportunity to hear and see for themselves the saving grace and mercy of God.

This Gospel attests that all we need is the charge. The authority. That what we need in order to spread the Gospel is ourselves. You know we have that authority. That we can and are charged with spreading the Gospel. The good news.

But, this Gospel doesn't tell us that everyone must be an outspoken evangelist. It doesn't say that everyone will immediately be changed. But what it does tell us is that we must be in the presence of others showing what the love of God and Jesus can do.

But, that being said, I'd also tell you that the Gospels do not say to hide the truth simply because that truth is sometimes hurtful to those who do not wish to hear it. I'd also tell you that the Gospels do not say to not hold others to accountability. You see the Gospels, this one in particular, can be harsh.

So, it seems that some of the real choices are that we can ignore the proverbial gorilla walking among us or stop and relook and re-listen to our own relationships and open our eyes and ears to what's being said to us, deep within us.

The parable illustrates that many people refuse to hear what is the truth and what is this world's lies. It shows two people that went down the same path. However, one of them went voluntarily and the other was led down that path by the evil of the brother. We can too.

We can lead others by our actions and by our inactions both. The trick, as illustrated, is to allow those who can't hear the good news to finally be informed by us of that good news so that all can live according to the will of God.

FAITH

Faith

Gospel – Mark 4:26 – 34

References – Psalm 78; Isaiah 6:9; Daniel 4; 2nd

Corinthians 12; Romans 3

There once was a king who built great walls. Not only did he build these walls, some reaching heights of 1,000 feet or more, around his castle but he proceeded to build them all around the borders of his kingdom. He told his subjects they were for their protection against any enemies that wanted to invade their lands.

However, he told himself it was to keep himself safe. Safe from anything that might cause him harm.

Now, this kingdom was not small. It spanned miles and miles of land and reached to opposing shores. It was so vast that it would take a person walking 100 days to cross it from east to west and 150 days to cross it from north to south.

After many, many years of building, the king lay on his death bed. He confided that the real purpose for the walls was not to keep others out but to keep everyone in. The real purpose was to have control over everyone's lives so that no harm could come to them.

But the real purpose was to define just who was in and who was out. In other words, who was acceptable to be a part of the family of the kingdom and, thereby, exclude those who didn't measure up.

****

In the old days, in many communities, generations lived in the same home. Children witnessed firsthand several generations. Learned from them and carried on certain family traditions. Today, our kids are raising themselves. Living out adult lives in children's bodies. This has resulted in a generation that some have called the lost generation.

Thomas Aquinas once wrote on faith and God that "To one who has faith, no explanation is necessary. To one without faith, no explanation is possible." The Gospel message really boils down to faith. What is it? Can we get it? Can we get more of it? Can we lose it? Can one have more than another? Why have it? Is Aquinas right?

Jesus speaks in parables twice in this short passage. Both of them are about seeds. Seeds of faith. It's probably useful to understand the type of mustard seed that Jesus, and all those others that use this, is referring to.

The mustard seed that Jesus is referring to is the Mediterranean Black mustard seed. It's not the smallest of seeds but it's, never the less, the one most often used in the Old and New Testament when referring to something starting out small but growing to great heights.

The Jews of that time built their fences with local rocks, they would've put their gardens within that rock wall to keep animals and intruders from coming in and either destroying the garden within or taking from the garden. The mustard tree, if found within those rock walls would've been uprooted and thrown away at the first sight.

But, in reality, Jesus is the root of that tree. Spreading the roots of His message to all those who are outside the rock walls. He's asking His followers whether they see themselves within that rock wall, the walls of the church. Or, would they view themselves on the outside. Outside of the man-made wall.

It's said that this parable by Jesus was given to reassure the disciples that "the apparently insignificant results of Jesus' preaching are no measure by which to judge the greatness of

the Kingdom of God which He proclaims." For as St.
Augustine also wrote, "Faith is to believe what you do not see;
the reward of this faith is to see what you believe." It's this
faith that is the root that you don't see in the immediate but will
see the result as time passes and new beginnings are laid out.

The parable illustrates that our families are fluid. Our families
can expand. Our families can change. The belief on the faith
that we have been given by God is that which we can use to
help our families to grow in their recognition of life and
interactions between.

The parable illustrates that no matter how much protection we
may want to have to protect our families, they will always be
ruled by the timetable of God.

<u>FAITH</u>

Fruit of the Vine

Gospel – John 15:1 – 17

There once was a man who planted his garden each year. And each year very little grew. No matter what, it seemed, that he would do to help his plants grow they just sort of sprouted and then stayed that way and soon wilted and died.

One day, the man's neighbor happened by while the man was out there yelling at his plants due to his frustration. The neighbor took one look and told the man the reason that his plants had never and will never grow to fullness.

What the neighbor told this man was that each of his plants was spaced so far apart that the fertilizer that he put on them became diluted and none of it would reach the roots. That it's only through the fertilization of the roots that the plants can grow and it's only through the connection with other plants that they can truly flourish.

So it is with each of us. When we're alone then the words to encourage our vines to produce fruit become dried and brittle.

When we engage with other people then we are fed by their presence.

****

This is a hard Gospel, from John, to hear. I can sort of see that when I read passages such as "If you keep my commandments, you will abide in my love" and "You are my friends, if you do what I command you".

A cursory reading of this might lead one to ask several questions: What happens if I can't keep all the commandments? And if I can't keep all the commandments, am I no longer loved by God or Jesus or no longer his friend much less welcomed into Heaven? How does one do something in which even the slightest failure makes us unloved?

I mean, isn't that what this says? Even the disciples couldn't fully abide. Peter denied Him 3 times. Most of them deserted Jesus at the cross. They hid in the upper room. But I'm not a person that purposely violates the commandments. I don't kill anyone and I certainly don't steal from others. I don't put any God or anything as my God or above God. I certainly honor my father and mother. And I certainly wouldn't take the name of the Lord in vain. I'm a good person right?

Well, here's the bad news and the good news – the proverbial two sides of the coin.

Whenever we think ill towards another person – we have killed them. That's hard living in Chicago with the taxi cabs cutting you off or honking at you. Our how about the person with 12 items in a ten item or less line?

Whenever we take even an extra minute for lunch – we have stolen. Lunch taking too long. Belly full of really good Mexican food so you just sort of sit there.

Whenever we are envious – we are coveting. Shiny stuff is the key right? Taking the Lord's name in vain. How about hitting our finger with a hammer – colorful metaphors is what I call them.

Violating some of the 10 commandments is an everyday thing. But we have the grace that only comes with Jesus. We are the only faith that has that option. We are broken. We love that which is evil and hate that which is good. The ability to ask for forgiveness from God Himself and be assured that our faith, this grace, enables Him to grant that forgiveness.

So what does this passage really mean? – Well, that's the good news. The 1st thing is to look at the meaning of abide.

Abide, menos, in Greek means to remain or stay. Live. Dwell. Be connected. It appears more than 60 times from the Psalm in its context to 2nd John. When combined with love, as in "abide in my love" it takes on the form of actually living within Jesus – Connected with Jesus – Having Jesus in your heart.

If Jesus has loved us from the beginning – we cannot do anything but remain in His love. We will always be abiding in His love because it is His to give and not ours to escape from. Nothing we can do will separate us from that. In the history of scripture – God has always come to us.

Love is a very strange thing. It's freely given but often rejected. Many people have decided that they can do without God, or Jesus or the love they give so freely. They are so caught up with themselves – within themselves that they really don't even see themselves when they look at themselves in the mirror – they see what they want to see instead of what God sees.

Jesus' 2nd commandment is to love your neighbor as yourself. The last verse in this Gospel. Accept them for who they are rather than what they do. Accept them and invite them to be a part of this whole faith thing that gives the only way out from this world to the only way in to the kingdom. Reach out from within the four walls of the church to the four corners of our communities to those that seem to be searching aloud and those that are searching silently and maybe have even given up on the grace we innately know.

The cross that spans the great divide between the world we want to make as our own to the heavens that make the world we live in pale in comparison. The cross that has us on one side and God on the other and the hands of Jesus to lead us across. Guiding us. Walking with us.

What Jesus is commanding us to do is to go out and tell others of the good news of that cross. The grace that is the cross. He has chosen us for that. We are called to be the fruit from the vine of grace. The fruit that grows from the love that Jesus has living in our hearts. The fruit that is sweet to the taste of even those who see it as something that has to be earned. He has told us that we will not be alone in this quest. That whatever we ask of the Father in His name may be given.

You see, this passage tells us that if we open our eyes, our ears, our hearts to those around us, they will come, they will ask us something, they will inquire of what this fruit is all about. What this grace is. Who this God is. Who this Jesus is. Why would they need Him? What difference does it make?

Why is He so special? WHY can God and Jesus be relied upon to give grace so freely?

Some people ask - But what do we say to these other people? Jesus is telling us to just be ourselves - Let our hearts tell the story. Ask questions of them – let them lead you where they need to be. We may not see immediate results but the story – the fruit of the vine has been born in others. And through that love of Christ – we can all begin to spread His love, His acceptance, His grace and His words through us to the hearts of those who are hardened, the hearts of those broken, the hearts of those yearning for what they do not know they really want. The hearts of those who are searching for a place to finally rest. Through the love of Christ, we can bear fruit in others – fruit that will last.

The parable illustrates that we are all interconnected and must be because without that connection to others of God's creation, we wither because our own selves cannot sustain us in those time when the world is pounding on our hearts.

FAITH

Persistent Faith

Gospel – Matthew 15:10 – 28

References – Numbers 33:50-56

Many years ago, a young man sat in prison. Convicted on false testimony of his best friend. Months before this man was sentenced, he and his friend had gotten into a heated argument. The young man was trying to get his friend to stop the criminality of his life. That sooner than later, he would get caught and spend the rest of his life behind bars.

So, it was remarkable that this young man would be sent to prison for a crime he didn't commit. But attempts at having others see the truth of the crime went without success. The man's family regularly came to visit and would always tell the man to have faith. That the truth would be found out. But years went by and there didn't seem to be any relief in sight.

Finally, as his friend, the one who gave false testimony, lay on his death bed from another crime he had committed, through testing of the guys DNA, it was found that the man in prison was in there wrongly.

So, the man who had sat in prison for so many years finally
was set free. Exonerated. And the real truth of what happened
was finally revealed.

****

This Gospel is really two stories. The second one, the one
about the woman calling out Jesus and making Him change
His mind has been done before. It's probably one of the most
often heard ones. Matthew uses a Canaanite woman while the
same story, in Mark, uses a woman who was a
Syrophoenician by birth but referred to as a Greek.

Jesus wasn't even supposed to be in the area due to the
historical enmity between the people in that area and Israel.
No disciple had been there so they wouldn't have necessarily
have even heard of Jesus much less would have believed in
some Jewish Messiah to come.

There are two things that stand out about this second story
which begins on verse 21 and that's the words the woman
said, "Lord, Son of David" and the reference to dogs. You see,
what this woman said to Jesus must have caught His
attention.

This woman, who was from an area that surely had no disciple
come into it, somehow called out the very words that

recognized Jesus for whom He was, "Lord, Son of David". The foretold Jewish Messiah. Those very words that were prophesied thousands of years earlier.

By saying these words, this woman summed up all of the wisdom that even Jesus's own disciples seemed to have missed over and over and over again. She recognized that here was the real Messiah in her midst. A Canaanite woman who was viewed by others in her community as less than worthy.

The Israelites would have viewed this woman in the same manner. They held cultural views of others as less than human. Their Roman counterparts were extremely efficient at cutting off anyone who didn't fall into line with the emperor's personal agenda. And they viewed the Jews the same as the Jews viewed non-Jews.

You'd think that the Jews, of that time, would've had enough of the Romans calling them that derogatory name that they wouldn't do the same to others. But no one really learns from their mistakes, do we?

And because of that, Jesus changes His ministry from Israel alone to include all of us. Yea, Jesus didn't originally come for you and me, sitting here, but only for the Jews. The lost sheep of Israel.

It's because of this woman that you and me can worship and praise and share in the Eucharistic meal. It's because of this woman and her recognition of Jesus as the Messiah, the Christ, that we can celebrate His birth and His death and, most importantly, His resurrection.

The story of humanity. The story that tells us that what we put into our mouths, our hearts, may be one thing but what comes out is many times quite another.

Jesus never said we're not to judge what people do but what He's saying is that we cannot judge another person by who they are because we rarely portray who we are but who we want people to think or believe we are. Jesus judged many.

When the Jews would call the Gentiles dogs, they were blaspheming. They were defaming their neighbors and those neighbors were not in a position that afforded the title. So, Jesus is telling us to be careful in what we say. Be careful about what we put into our hearts.

The parable illustrates that it may take a while, but truth always wins out. Sometimes, it may come after a person is already dead but the truth always wins out. Sometimes others have to endure pain and hardship but the truth always wins out. Jesus tells us to have faith. I say, have belief in the faith that God has already given to you and, at least, you will have the strength to enable the truth to always win out.

FAITH

Understanding Reality

Gospel – John 3:1 – 21
References – Matthew 22

There once was a guy named Ted whose favorite line was, "Prove it. Show me." Everything anyone would tell him, he always came back to that phrase. It tended to irritate people because not everything could be proven or shown because not every bit of information was physical in nature.

Then one day, Ted lost his eyesight. Everything around him became dark and unknown. Ted could no longer rely on his pat answer of "Prove it. Show me" because Ted couldn't even begin to see it with his own eyes. Ted had to reassess what he wanted to believe to be aligned with what he believed he wanted to know.

Soon Ted would listen a bit more deeply to what someone had to say. Ted would analyze for the underlying truths rather than dismiss it altogether. Ted became more introspect out of necessity in order to function in his society.

Ted found out what most of those around him already knew. That the physical world in which you can see, touch, and smell was secondary to one's ability to explore the possibilities of what reality truly was and begin to believe in that reality.

****

Nichodemus, in this passage, was focusing in on the wrong thing. He was limiting Jesus to the earthly things. He was discounting all the miracles that he and his branch of Judaism had witnessed. He was concentrating on only that which he could see, touch and hear but ignoring the obvious higher things. He missed the rope and, as a result, fell deep into the abyss of misdirection.

A Pharisee of that time was an expert in the Law of Moses. They had dissected those Ten Commandments and expanded them to over 600. Jesus must have blown their minds when He reduced even those ten down to two.

But this Gospel goes even further than that. When Jesus is talking about being born of water and Spirit, He's not speaking of the physical. The water is Jesus and the Spirit is the Holy Spirit.

So what Jesus is talking about is believing in something that everyone else who only wants to prove the existence of this or that just cannot accept. That there are things of this world that transcend even our feeble ability to comprehend.

But understanding what Jesus is telling Nichodemus is like a parachutist. Belief is that the chute is packed correctly. That when you pull the cord that chute will open. That when you step off the plane, you, yourself, have done everything possible within your power to ensure that you don't fall 15,000 feet to your death. That is belief.

As Jesus was using the wind to illustrate His point to Nichodemus, those who believe only have to look at the life of Jesus and the kinds of things He did and the historical recordings of the thousands who saw Him after He was crucified. We can know beyond a shadow of doubt that the winds that Jesus is speaking about are very real despite the fact that we cannot actually see them but can only see the result of them.

When Jesus is speaking to Nichodemus, Nichodemus is illustrating the fears and irrational belief that we all have. It's hard for us to get a real grip on what a rebirth is. Jesus is not laying down a new law. After all, He said that He didn't come to abolish the law but to fulfill it.

Jesus is expressing to Nichodemus the futility of hanging on to earthly things as they will soon wither and die. Jesus is telling us the same thing.

The parable illustrates to us that everything that we can believe in is not necessarily everything we can see, touch and hear. God's majesty is always showing us that there is more to what is around us than we can even begin to understand. Jesus is telling Nichodemus that he is like Ted in that it is time he got past what was limited in his vision and really open his eyes to the possibilities backed by the truth of Jesus. The parable tells us that if we can begin to let go then Jesus puts so much more at our senses than we could possibly imagine.

FAITH

We Are Remade

Gospel – John 1:42 – 51

There once was a man whose life had been one of strict religious upbringing which led him to shy away from pretty much any negative encounter that he might cause to another. He would avoid confrontations and walk away when cornered.

As he got older, he worked at a shipyard and saw his future in that capacity. But war broke out and he was enlisted. His religious background forbade him from carrying any weapons and he caught all kinds of grief and persecution from his fellow soldiers. He was even given the opportunity to resign. But he refused and became a medic.

It was when he was in battle in the Philippines, saving the lives of over 100 of his fellow soldiers, that he was also wounded four times with multiple shrapnel embedded in his body. Once the war was over, he came back to the states, married and had a son. But his wife died in a car accident a few years later while he was driving. He couldn't save her but he did save 100s of others.

Who he became was a result of who he was which is defined by who he was in his past. Every person is reshaped into avenues for greater glory and purpose even if they don't know it. Some use that opportunity to become something that brings life to others. Some bypass that opportunity and those around them suffer because of that decision too.

****

Jesus comes to each of us at different times in our lives. For some, He comes and knocks and they hear Him for the very first time. For others, they have a much closer relationship with Him and they seem to hear Him over and over. But, you can bet, each of us will hear Him at some point in our lives.

When Jesus met up with Simon and renamed him Cephas, or Peter, Jesus was doing more than just giving him a nickname. Jesus was renaming Simon to give Simon a purpose for his life. His renaming was just a start to what He saw as the future for all of us sitting in churches everywhere.

Jesus was remaking Simon to be a person that could see his own potential that might have been hidden. Jesus took Simon and reimagined him to be a leader. We're not sure the past of Simon but we certainly know his future.

But Simon wasn't the only one whom Jesus went to and targeted that person's future. Shaped that future. Nathaniel and Thomas were two others. Jesus showed the both of them the real truth of the matter, Nathaniel by the fig tree and Thomas the intimate parts of His crucifixion that answered the overriding questions that they both had about their present and, most importantly, their future.

That's the way it was with Simon. But it went even further. Because Simon was to head this new group of believers, his position has directed everything theological, or church wise, from that time forward. In other words, almost all of the things that we do today, observe today, act on today are, in some shape, formed by what Simon decided what must be done 2,000 plus years ago.

But it also displays, or illustrates, something more. It shows that Jesus remakes all of us into what He needs us to be whether we know it or not. Whether we really get it or not. Whether we accept it or not.

But, we kind of do the same thing with our own kids too. I mean, haven't you just told your child something and then think to yourself, I'm sounding more and more like my father or mother every day. We tend to try and shape our kids into our own image of what we want them to be.

And sometimes our children have a hand in remaking us. Things we see that were hidden seem to be illustrated to us by those smallest around us. Those that view life and purpose in a simpler context. Jesus tries to keep it simple too. After all, He took hundreds of rules and laws that came from the Ten Commandments and reduced them down to just two.

Jesus comes to us and makes it simple for us. He takes what we are and remakes us into something worthy for the Father. He allows us to make our own choices in the hopes that we can follow His script for our future. But just as Jesus remakes us, each of us sees something unique in Jesus because of that remaking.

But who we determine Jesus to be is who we will be because He's within us. Filling our individual needs for challenges that'll happen. Giving us the ammunition that we'll need in order to do battle with the evils of this world. Enabling us to be a new person that can cut through all the bull we hear to get down to the truth of whatever comes into our view.

The parable illustrates that each of us contributes to others in ways that sometimes cannot be immediately seen or felt but the actions we take impacts never the less.

The man in the parable was not a fighter but his desire to serve helped him to overcome the negativity of his peers. And that saved them because he used his talents in other ways. We can do the same because not every one of us is made the same. We are made in the image of God and, as such, our roads are set forth by God. Some travel down those roads and some get caught in the rut. Our choice is to follow or get lost.

<u>FORGIVENESS</u>

Shortchanging Forgiveness

Gospel – Matthew 18:21 – 35
References – Genesis 4:15, 24; 1st Corinthians 13:5;
Ephesians 4:3 – 4; Philippians 2:2

There once was an old man who would never leave his house. No matter how many of his friends would drop by to invite him out, not only wouldn't he leave but he wouldn't even invite them in. This went on for some time but it wasn't always like that.

The old man used to participate in the town parades and help out in the soup kitchen for years in his community. He would volunteer to take turkeys to those who couldn't afford one on Thanksgiving and served as a Santa during the Christmas season.

Then, one day, he stopped coming. He stop volunteering. He stopped serving. It seemed that everyone wanted to know where he was and what had happened. They knew he hadn't died so they were curious.

When his friends finally did get the old man to tell them what was going on, he told them that he had accidentally hit the neighbor's dog one day while out driving. And then, if that wasn't bad enough, he had told that neighbor that it was a stranger driving through.

He felt that, with the accident and the lying that he did, no one would want him around anymore. His friends told him that the dog he had hit had survived and was regularly seen outside playing with the kids and that the lie he had told could be, and was, overlooked. Forgiven.

Forgiven because the neighbor had known all along that it was him, not a stranger, but didn't hold any grudge against him because they knew it wasn't on purpose but was a simple accident.

****

Forgiveness. It's something that's so easy to say when there's no pressure or it's about someone else doing the forgiving. But, when it comes to us, personally, it becomes a bit more harder. Sometimes it seems it can never be given.

Sometimes, it's all we can do to just look at the other person in the eyes and consider them to be a friend again. A relative again. A close brother or sister or parent again.

But, sometimes, when we do forgive, it seems that an awfully heavy weight has been lifted from our souls, lifted from our hearts, and the end result is that it almost always seems that sense of fresh air fills the room, if not our general demeanor.

Holding a grudge can be an awful heavy burden and tends to color every aspect of our lives. Darkens everything we look at and everything we pursue. We have those occasions come up and the non-forgiveness of whom-ever clouds our relationships with literally every person we're around.

So, the forgiveness that Jesus is speaking about here between each of us goes deeper. Deeper than any of us can imagine. Deeper, I'd guess, than any of us can or, at times, wish to do. It's interesting to note that Peter, himself, needed forgiveness from Christ seven times.

But, forgiving doesn't mean that you must purge your memory of the action taken against you. The mind is not designed that way. No, forgiveness isn't about forgetting but rather what we do with our hearts. How we allow what happened to us to affect our inner most being and, as a result, affect how we view and treat our brothers and sisters.

But we're not told that we must draw a blank slate toward the person committing the offense. We're just not supposed to hold onto that deed like an internal savings account. Always going back in to see how much it's grown.

Forgiveness doesn't always entail reconciling with our offender. We're not required to go face to face with them in order to forgive them. Reconciliation may be desirable, as an example, with a close relative or with your mother or father or sister or brother, but it's not required. But, reconciliation isn't always possible though because it requires a mutuality that just may not be possible. It requires repentance.

But, when we're going person to person, who we forgive cannot be measured by how much we must be forgiven. That's like keeping score and it truly means there's been no forgiveness. No reconciliation. I do know that simply forgiving does not mean forgetting. Removing that incident from our minds.

The parable illustrates that forgiveness to be had is sometimes hard to take from someone who wants to give it. The forgiveness that Jesus is speaking of was hard because it required people to grow out of themselves and clear their conscious so that grace and replace that hatred or hurt.

The parable illustrates that sometimes we're the hardest on ourselves and do not allow others to forgive us. Jesus says to accept it and we're on way to living as the child of God we are.

<u>FUTURE</u>

Our Stones that Cause Us to Stumble

Gospel – Matthew 16:21 – 28

References – Proverbs 2:8; 2nd Corinthians 4; Revelations 22:15 – 16

There once was a guy who thought he was pretty handy around the house. He would get it in his mind that this or that needed fixing and he was just the guy to get it done. So, he would go get all the supplies. Go get all the tools. Set aside the time during his busy week. And then he would begin the project that he wanted to get done.

But he always just threw away the instructions on the part to be installed or repaired and also the instructions on the tools to do the project and, as a result, something would invariably go wrong or he couldn't replace a needed part on the tool he was using. He just could figure it out.

But, had this guy taken the time to read all the instructions on the assembly rather than just look at the pictures, taken the time to understand how the tool worked and how to repair it, he would've saw where the final pieces would fit together and he might have been more successful in completing what he started.

This tends to apply to many of the people walking around. They jump to conclusions about something they only half saw or they come to a belief in half of the information they heard. Then people cannot seem to accept when they're wrong and their mindset becomes fixed. Or broken. Or not completed. Like the projects the guy wanted to complete.

****

You know, Jesus is telling you and me to stop thinking of heaven as the end goal and look at all that's around you as the disciple you were created to be and let being the disciple be the goal.

Change our thinking from our human standards, something we can measure, and begin to live it as God's divine revelation. Move those road blocks that we invariably put into our paths that hamper our understanding and our relationship that we can have with God that are put there by others and by yourselves to make you stumble.

Those stones that we have are the same as the ones the disciples had. They're all the crap that we're faced with in this world on a day to day basis. They're the news we hear that everything is going to Hell in a handbasket. They're the violence and evil that slaps us in the face almost every moment we're awake.

Our future is in the hands of our God. Now and forever. The desires we have are always less than the pure results that can be created by our God. Now and forever. The lives that we want for ourselves always comes up shorter than the ones that are designed for us by the hands of our God. Now and forever.

This Gospel is about who do you really believe and truly know as the one who came to rule over you. Who do you accept as the reality of today that can give you the strength to see things clearly so much so that all that news can be seen for what it really is, a temporary time in which some delude themselves into believing that they're invincible and have complete control over what comes next.

So it is with us. When we allow all the minutia of what we see and hear to create fear and uncertainty in our lives, keep us apart from each other, look at others with suspicion because they're not following what leaders have mandated, then we've kept the sunlight from our own lives that would allow us to reach for the heavens because everything I've just mentioned becomes just another stone that we've unwittingly placed on our own roads of life.

So, Jesus is telling every one of us, sitting here, that to fulfill His mission is to be His mission. Jesus is telling every one of us, sitting here, that to be able to complete the project we gotta look at what He's saying to us.

The parable illustrates that like the gardens of our lives, so it is with the guy in the parable. By only looking at the picture of what the project was supposed to end up like, He's put road blocks in the way to impede completion of that project. By not reading all the instructions given with the tools, He's left out important information that would allow Him to repair or move those road blocks so that the project could be completed. So that our lives can be complete.

FUTURE

Promise of the Holy Spirit

Gospel – John 15:18 – 27; 16:4 – 15

References – Leviticus 23

There once was a young man who lost his father. The young man was by his father's side every day and even sat by his side while at the hospital living out the last of his days. In the bed next to the young man's father lay another man whose days were numbered.

The other man would cry out frequently and constantly showed great pain. The young man's father lay quietly and remembered all the good memories and the family that he had that were close. He rested with comfort.

The man in the neighboring bed would shout out about those in his family that he had wronged. He would cry out for all the pain he had caused them. No one came to visit the man in agony. No one came to sooth his conscience. No one seemed to care about his last days.

The young man thought it odd that this man should be so alone. So, while he was tending to his own father who was at peace with his life, the young man would try to comfort the other man. Soon enough both died.

The young man's father drifted off into a peace filled eternity. The neighbor man was, himself, finally at peace too because of the young man's comfort.

If only each of us could walk past our own pain to see the other side. If only each of us could come out of ourselves and help others to know they are loved too.

****

The Holy Spirit moves when God speaks. It kind of does the work of God. He says it, the Spirit goes to work. Much like when your boss says to go do something and then you do it. But we consider the Holy Spirit to be a part of the Trinity don't we?

Luther wrote that the Holy Spirit teaches, preaches and declares Christ. The Holy Spirit is the only one that's able to say: Jesus Christ is the Lord and it's through the Holy Spirit working through us that we are able to declare that too.

In this passage from John, John uses the word Advocate for the Holy Spirit. The word Advocate has many meanings – it goes by the Hebrew Paraclete, which means helper, counselor, intercessor, or comforter among many other things.

John is unique in that he is using the Advocate as Jesus so that the followers would be able to keep Jesus alive and with them after He was gone. When Jesus left, it left a really big hole for His followers.

They no longer had a physical presence to look up to, to talk to, to be near to. By substituting this Advocate for Jesus, it gave them something they could cling to. But Jesus is telling His disciples that the Holy Spirit will come down on them, descend on them, like a bull in a china closet. That they must have this in order to carry on with their mission.

Now we come to church. Hear the good news. Talk among ourselves. And then go back into that big wide world. Most of the time, church is left at the door. John is saying that we can take Jesus with us every day. That we must take Jesus with us every day. In every situation. In every place.

I believe that God speaks through the Holy Spirit to us if we can just quiet the world around us long enough that we can hear Him. I have said to others and I will probably be repeating myself but I believe that you know when the Holy

Spirit is talking to you when He answers your questions to Him before you finish the question.

Technically, Pentecost is defined as 50 days after Easter or the 7th Sunday. It's the Jewish Feast of Weeks or Harvest as spelled out in Leviticus 23. In other words the feast of the first fruits. We are those first fruits.

Pentecost is marked by 3 events – Winds of the Holy Spirit, Fire on the tongues of the disciples as it was in the burning bush, and then speaking in other unknown languages by the disciples.

But many denominations believe that the days of speaking in tongues and other things the disciples did is over. They call that the end of the Apostolic age. They say that it ended around 100AD since no new revelation had emerged. On the other end of the spectrum are those that believe that there never was an end to this age and are most often seen to show off their supposed gift of tongue and healing practices.

Scripture tells us that the Disciples would speak in tongues. But what is also shown is that in order for that speaking to be valid, there must be another to interpret it. And that it cannot be a tongue that is foreign to absolutely everyone present.

So the gifts that we receive from God, Jesus and the Holy Spirit may not be those of the Apostles but they are gifts never the less. We can see it in other people most of all. Like when you see a great baseball player and you hear "He's a natural" or "They were born to do this".

I believe that we're in a new Apostolic age of sorts. I see it in the growth of churches but I also see how that Spirit is corrupted by many faith traditions. But I am quite sure that God will do as God wants to do.

Unfortunately, most do not see a grace filled God but, rather, an envious God. A God that throws down good people into bad things. A God that is my way or the by way. A God that is jealous. But those are human devices that simplify God to our level of understanding.

The parable illustrates the possibility that we can go beyond ourselves to help others when they are in pain. It also shows that how we live our days will be how we spend our last minutes on the earth. Those who had only lived for themselves will see themselves alone and forgotten. Those who had lived for others will find themselves accompanied throughout those last minutes. One is painful. The other glorious.

<u>HEALING</u>

Challenges

Gospel – Mark 5:21 – 43

References – Leviticus 15; Deuteronomy 32:39; Matthew 7

There once was a man that it seemed that everything he did, nothing would turn out good. He found himself a new job after months of being unemployed only to have the company go out of business a couple of months later. He found himself the girl of his dreams only to have her fall in love with another man a couple of months later. He had finally bought himself his dream home but had to go into foreclosure because he had lost his job.

So, nothing he did, he felt, ever came out right and he was always clawing to keep his head above the waters. But then he walked into a store that had just opened up out of curiosity since it said it sold things that no one else in the town did.

When he walked in, he noticed that the shelves were in great disarray. He met the store owner who was so ragged from the opening that the owner could barely keep awake. So, the man offered his help and it was accepted.

The man spruced up the store. Made it so that new customers could both find what they wanted and had information on newer items that they didn't even know they wanted. And they bought those. Months went by and the store prospered.

The relationship between the man and the store owner blossomed. She was just his type. She also offered the man to be part owner of the store due to his efforts and knowledge of what the customers wanted.

The man found that only through taking a chance on something he could not have dreamed of, the man finally found his permanent place in the world and him and the woman, who was now his bride, saw that when one challenge seems too much, it's really only pointing you to a path to success.

****

So, when you're faced with a challenge, what do you do? Many face it head on, work to overcome it, and learn from any failures that might arise. Others just run the other way. Many seek others to help them. Many more take the Lone Ranger approach and try to do it themselves. Many climb the tree of progress to reach the level where they can see the challenge in a clear light. Many more react like the fox towards the grapes in that tree in the old Aesop's fable and give up.

The Gospel is just about that and the very two different people that sought a solution to their two very different but similar problems. You see, the two people in this passage are both suffering.

The social stations were that the bleeding woman became a lower class person due to her affliction, the girl's father was of a higher class due to his position. And each must reach out to the one they know deep within is the only one that can give them what it is that can relieve their pain and suffering, Jesus. You see, at that present point in time, both the woman and Jairus are equal in stature before God and the grace of Jesus and they both faced challenges to their own lives because of the social stations they were in.

But sometimes we seek the wrong help in the wrong ways from the wrong people in the wrong places while ignoring good advice or help simply because we don't see the solution to our challenge that the other might know. Sometimes we want to believe that we can solve all of our problems, all of our challenges, ourselves.

You see, it's not the challenges we face that define us but in how we go about dealing with them and who we put our trust in to lead us over those challenges. In this passage, both main characters chose to take an action. The positive result wasn't that they took that action but in how they chose to believe in how the results, the results of their requests, would turn out.

Jairus and the woman both allowed their faith in the one that could provide relief to precede their requests. Jairus and the woman both realized that it wasn't what they brought with them, their money or power or even the actual affliction, that would make the difference. And Jairus and the woman didn't have any guarantee that what they wanted, what they believed would cure their ails, would result in the expected outcome.

I'm reminded by the passage in this Gospel that even the lowest of low in societies ranking and the highest on high both have to come to the middle, preceded by faith, to receive the blessings and the cure that Jesus is there waiting to give. Their faith precluded their healing. Our faith also is the first step to healing whatever we're dealing with.

Jesus deals with us one to one. In our silence. In our ailments. In our troubles. He walks with us as we traverse our challenges and He helps us to overcome those same challenges bit by bit.

The parable illustrates that we all go through times in our lives where it may seem that the roadblocks are just too high. That the obstacles are too much. That the world is pressing down and all the bad is starting to close in on us.

The man in the parable would not know that his future was right around the corner. It took all the disappointments that he had to point him in a new life. We can be that same way. Allow everything to keep us down. Jesus says it is our belief that gives us hope. It is our belief gives us the way out.

<u>HEALING</u>

On First Blush

Gospel – Mark 1:21 – 28

A man walks into a local Goodwill store and begins to look around. After about five minutes, his eyes land on an old clock sitting on a mantle up against a wall in the corner of the store. It was very dirty and had a lot of cob webs hanging on it. It looked like it had been sitting there for a very long time.

When he asked the clerk, behind the counter, about it, the clerk told him that he really didn't have much information about it since it had been sitting in that exact spot ever since the store opened. The store had been owned by a very old lady who said it was a store her grandfather opened just after the depression. They had sold homemade items from local crafts persons. So, the clock probably was from that time.

But the man had recognized the clock as an old shelf clock that was made in New England back in the 19th century by the Willards. The clock was very valuable because of its historical and craftsmanship value.

The world's time had hidden the internal intricacies of the item's value with ugliness and it took someone who knew its innate value to bring out the beauty of that work.

****

This Gospel, from Mark, is Jesus taking the raw and making it smooth. He takes the evil out of the man. The evil that had taken over that man. He went into battle for the guy, and came out on top. He does the same with you and me too. In the process, he showed those, which were witnessing this, that He was the real deal.

You know, we could use Him today, in our world, right about now too. Not just the spiritual side but Jesus on the physical side that's an in your face sort of truth that can't be swept under the rug with a nice motto or a politically correct phrase or a narrative.

Maybe history will repeat itself in that the folks today will simply discount Him today as they did then. Maybe the folks today will call Him a racist or a xenophobe because He'd say there's only one road to heaven and it's through Him. Maybe he'll get banned from all major media platforms because He is divisive. Maybe he'll be excluded from all the non-cis gendered gatherings because He isn't fluid in His own gender identity.

Now, in Jesus' day, Capernaum was a hub of activity. Guys would gather in the temple to hear the words of the prophets and go home every night to a depression because the time hadn't come yet. So when Jesus came in and rebuked the demon, a light went off and that put a major cramp in the ruling class of the day. Truth has a way of doing that. The evil then and the evil today has a tendency to hide from the truth. Can't stand the light.

The craziest part of it all is that the people there were amazed. I mean, didn't they even listen to what the prophets had told them was gonna happen? The prophets said that the Messiah would come and He'd have control over all these evil demons and take control over all mankind. They were pretty clear about that.

You know, we, as believers, have an enormous task ahead of us. For every one of those that truly believe there are six or eight others that have either relegated Jesus to some cute bedtime story or those that have said that unless He conforms to what we want Him to be then He mustn't be real.

But, I do know that Jesus directly assaulted the established orders of the day and He's kinda doing the same thing today. He's calling all of us to look past the regulations and theocratic bull crap that has built up over the centuries to keep you in line with whatever the church fathers thought and, instead, invites you to take another look at who this Jesus was and is.

I do know that the nature of the kingdom is such that it provokes antagonism that divides audiences into insiders who can perceive the truth of the eternal message versus outsiders who want Him to be who they want Him to be even if it goes against what's written.

After all, did any of us who were born before 1960 ever think that kids could be bullied electronically and they would take it seriously? Do any of us pre-1960s kids ever think that there would be those who are famous simply because they're famous not because they actually did anything but because they got a lot of likes on social media? Do any of us pre-1960s kids choose to have a conversation that's entirely on some screen and then take seriously what someone wrote?

You see, like the clock on the mantle and the guy in the attic, our first blush of reality is really determined by the truth surrounding our own desires and how well we accept and incorporate that truth.

The parable illustrates that just as the clock sits on the mantle in our parable gathering dust, we too can gather dust out of fear or uncomfortableness. It's our time to dust that thing of beauty off, our belief in our faith, and strike out for a new time.

A time where people can gather and be welcomed home. A time where we can gather the courage and tell even one other person of the Good News. A time where we can gather and pray that the whole truth and nothing but the truth so help me God will boil to the top and those that have set their roots in convenience will find they can plant anew.

HEALING

Status Quo Rebellion

Gospel – Mark 1:29 – 45
References – Mark 5

There once was a young man who had an extremely difficult childhood. His mother was 14 when she had him and he never knew his father. The child was dyslexic and made fun of at school so much so that he dropped out in his junior year.

The young man wandered about and met up with others that were on the fringe of society. They convinced others to join their group and they set up camp preaching that the end of days were near. This young man was very convincing to many and, as a result, recruits came from as far away as Australia.

In the beginning, the young man and his followers were, as far as anybody could tell, law abiding. Peaceful. But, as time went on, the young man had visions of grandeur and declared himself to be the new Messiah and proceeded to project this image, of himself, to quite a few gullible converts. He claimed for himself the grandeur that was reserved for the one he was supposed to abide in and, instead, became a symbol of darkness for many.

The end came when the rantings of this man ran afoul of the law of the land and the end result was that most, if not all, of those followers were violently killed. The man had claimed he was the gift from God as the messiah whereas the real gift from God never claimed it for Himself.

The real Messiah, as in all the prophets before, allowed the people they helped to see the beauty of the truth and the people proclaimed them Messiah.

****

You know what I think is probably one of the most fascinating things about the Gospel stories and all those others in the New Testament? It's that they're about one guy and all those who chose, out of their own freewill, to drop everything and follow Him. About how the hundreds would go to their deaths just because their belief was so strong.

And, for all the real Messiah's follower's troubles, they were persecuted but what they held deep within their hearts is that the one that they had been promised had finally come and given them a new guide to go by. They put it out there so that we could gather today because without them, we wouldn't probably even know about this Messiah.

So it is with us. Perseverance. Keep looking towards the truth. You know folks, the fact of the matter is that the truth about this whole faith thing is that each of us living today has that same level of faith. We can't get more of it because it was given by God as a gift. We can't lose it because it's a part of our DNA.

You know, it was common knowledge, back then, that charismatic figures gathered crowds in deserted places in order to start rebellions. Physical rebellion as the Jews did shortly after Jesus was crucified. But Jesus never preached rebellion unless it was against the demons that were believed to live within people. Took control of people.

The people sought out Jesus. They sought Him out just like God seeks us out. Where we are. In whatever place we may be. God seeks us out. The main reason, I believe, is that we're all looking for that little piece of truth. The real stuff. The real McCoy. Not the stuff we're fed with on a day to day basis. But the real, unmitigated truth that we know is right because it reaches that part in us all that's crying out to hear it.

The demons that He cast out? Those were the barriers that we all have to hearing what Jesus has in store for us. We're all surrounded by demons. Not necessarily the ones that are what you see that's made into movies but the ones that hold us back through the fear that we all have of the unknown. That daily stuff that seems to be such a high barrier to cross over.

When the leper said to Jesus, "If You are willing, You can make me clean." He's saying that Jesus is the Son of God because only the Son of God can command it and it gets done. And all those folks who were at the door, watching and waiting for either confirmation or their turn, they recognized what and who Jesus was too.

The journey of our lives and how it interacts with others is a testimony to our own fears of not being all we can be. But, more importantly, it's a testimony that with the belief that's to be firmly planted in the arms of God, it becomes a testimony to our character not only for ourselves but to all others who are looking for that light too. The darkness cannot overcome the light.

But like the darkness that invades our minds, it can take over our very consciousness, create and aggravate the fear that's innate in all of us. It cannot sustain itself if we'll just let that light shine in. Let the light of Jesus come into your hearts so that it overpowers and crowds out all the negativity, which is the darkness.

The parable illustrates that there are guys, like the one in our parable, who had taken that belief, that hope, and turned it around for their own benefit. Their own misguided desire to be elevated above everyone else with some special insight as to what was gonna happen tomorrow when, in fact, none of us knows for sure what tomorrow will bring or even if we'll still be on this side of the concrete. The guy in our parable believed himself to be the one whom God had made the exception for. The one God gave all the answers too. At least that's what he portrayed to his followers.

<u>HEAVEN</u>

Our Ethics in the Light of God

Gospel – Matthew 25:31 – 46

References – Revelations 1:3

It was a Thanksgiving like any ordinary Thanksgiving in many years past in many houses across this nation. The family and relatives had all come together. Hugs were given, stories were shared, and everyone always laughed at the grumpy uncle who was forever telling the worst jokes. Then they all sat down to dinner at the very long table with the short card table at the end for the kids.

But this Thanksgiving a special guest has arrived after everyone has already been seated and had just started to carve the turkey. This guest is someone that everyone thought they knew but couldn't quite remember where or when they came to know of Him. This guest is dressed in rags but there is just something regal about Him. This guest starts to sit down at the end of the table with the kids. The children.

Immediately, Grandma gets up to offer Him her seat at the head but he chooses to remain at the end of the lowest table, with the innocence of the children. Everyone looks at Him while searching back in their memory of just who He is. Some have a vague recollection of hearing of Him when they were children in church but weren't sure. Some remembered Him right away but then also remember that they have put that memory of Him so far back that the everyday things and deals and responsibilities moved into His place.

And then this guest starts to speak. Softly at first, so much so that only those closest to Him can hear Him. Hear His quiet tale of telling the story of how He had come to know each of the people there.

He tells of seeing them walk by as he was sitting on the street corner remembering how He sat with them when they were hurt. He tells of hearing them talking above and around Him but never to Him even though they knew each other very well years before. He tells of missing the touch of each of them even though, years before, they regularly reached out for Him.

With each of these stories, His voice becomes louder and more pronounced. More and more of the people at the head of the table, the far end away from Him, are beginning to hear Him and what they hear makes them very uncomfortable.

Not because the stories are vague or insulting or anything like that but because they are true and personable and hits them in their hearts and their memory banks that they had all locked up all those years before because they wanted to fit in with the world around them. Hide their pains. Ignore that little voice that's calling out to each of them.

****

Our memories become challenged with time. They're filled with all sorts of expectations that sometimes lives up to what's wanted but sometimes aren't what we expected. But that's OK since we think to ourselves that we're just grateful to be able to have people around. It's important to keep those who cannot have loved ones around in our hearts and our prayers during this time.

The very first settlers on this land, almost 30 years prior to the one we celebrate, had a very much different outcome. This was a group that landed at Jamestown and was the very first socialistic experiment in this new land. Everyone there worked for the central committee. All crops were assigned by this central group. All harvests were given over to the central group and then a portion was allotted out to each evenly. Not according to what was brought in but evenly. The same.

The problem was that this led to inadequacies in what was needed by each individual family. This led to a very human desire to rule. To exert absolute power. The basic needs of each settler was measured by the whole and not the individual. Jesus, in this Gospel, assigns those people in such positions of authority to the left, with the goats.

The end result was that of the original 104 colonist, 15 years later on, only 23 were still alive including most of the central committee members, interesting enough. Many starved to death. Many died from the elements. Many from disease brought on by lack of desire to actually work because they were promised their lives would be taken care of.

The second try, at Plymouth, they changed their tactics and determined that each future settler could plant what they wanted or needed and then sold or traded to the other colonists. The very first capitalist society on this continent as the result was not without hardship but it became fruitful. They still needed help from the natives and they were spurred on with that sense of individual assistance to accept that help and, as a result, survived and thrived.

You see, with the first group, the Jamestown group, anyone who was in need, was hungry, was thirsty, was supposedly looked out for by the central committee, not the individuals as the rule, but the central committee was never designed to take care of any individual specifically. It was set up to turn a blind eye to the individual in lieu of the collective.

But Jesus is saying just the opposite. He's saying that the individual has the ethical duty and obligation to take on the hardships of our neighbors. What counts is our ethics in relation to God's ultimate creation, us. The central committee was never God's creation but ours. God specifically warned against such a system. Saul, in the Old Testament, was such a creation by the Jews of that day.

Ethics is defined as the moral principles that govern a person's behavior or the conducting of an activity. It can be extended to all aspects of our lives and how we contribute to or take away from our communities. It's ultimately the self-giving care for others that's at the heart of the revealed will of God in the Torah.

It asks us to ask ourselves, who are the relations, who are the least of these, do we look at those who see themselves as outsiders as really within the walls of God's kingdom, and how do we define the needy.

The Gospel points out to us, especially in the troubling times we're living in, that those that have replaced His words with the kingdom of this world will be put with the goats on the left.

The parable illustrates that Jesus is coming to your table. He has always been coming to your table. He will forever always come to your table. Open your eyes, your ears, your tongue to welcome Him into your realities. Grab that person who sits next to you and welcome them into the family of God. We are one in the same family.

<u>HEAVEN</u>

Systemic Humanism and Humanity

Gospel – Matthew 18:15 – 20

References – Leviticus 19:17 – 18; Deuteronomy 19:15;

Galatians 6:2; 2nd Thessalonians 3:14 – 15

There once was a man who would regularly attend football games with his "Go Packers" Wisconsin t-shirt and cap on. Then he would be one of the loudest people there when the Packers were playing and his yelling for that team.

Everyone who would come up to him, he would go on and on about how the Packers were sent by the almighty, himself, to vanquish all those that went against them. When he was in line at the concession stand, he would always ask for a basket of cheese curds and some booyah stew.

All this, this man would do, no matter where he went or who he met in the stadium and always proclaimed these things at the top of his voice for all to hear. Many would shy away from him and try not to get too close.

Now, all this would be fine except that this man lived in Minnesota and always went to the Vikings games. And, it seems, no one would point this very fact to him and how it affected all those people that were standing around him. They would just talk among themselves. And scowl at him.

****

Jesus lays it on the line here. He says that if one of you, or me, becomes offended with someone else, we're supposed to go talk to that person, in person, and, if that doesn't help, then we're supposed to go get two others to go back with us to that person to address the offense.

And if that doesn't solve the problem, then we're supposed to get ourselves and the other person in front of the whole church and let the whole church decide the outcome of the offense.

It seems, more often than not, that what really happens is that whispers are said and then more whispers and then more whispers and so on and so on. And after a couple of rounds of those, the damage has already been done and it's irreparable.

Jesus is saying that in order to keep this family of faithful together there must be open communication between all the people and it's the church itself that makes the final determination as to whether the offending party should just get over themselves or whether there's merit to what they're claiming.

That's hard to do today in our society where we can cancel someone out from behind the safety of anonymity. Behind the keyboard of a phone or a computer. In the so-called back alleys where the light of truth is hard to see. Where attitudes are created based on lies and deceit.

This passage is about how some may want to bring ideas that are contrary to scripture into the house that God built and alter the way that His word is given and what can be said or done while we're here. It's about community and how the community can hold each other in communion with each other. Lift each other up.

When there are factions claiming, or yelling, that this society is systemic what-ever, then they're attempting to exert some control over the society that they're yelling at because if they're successful, then they've become the very one that oppresses because they've taken the freedom, in how ever way, from the person they claim is the oppressor.

This whole systemic thing is also anti-theological in its foundation because it assumes the worst about a person or culture when we're called by God, himself, to believe the best.

It puts people into a classification that someone on the outside wants to polarize to make that person fit or be what the claimer claims they are.

But it goes further because it's the ultimate in self-adoration that elevates one person, the one making the claim, to a position to judge the character of any whom they desire or dislike.

Which brings us back to the passage at hand. What Jesus is saying is that the only systemic thing in the history of all of us is our inability to follow what it is that He's telling the disciples, and us, here to do. Work with each other. Be at peace with each other.

The parable illustrates that our own ideas and the veracity that we hold to those ideas tends to shout down those with competing ideas. This results in hearts and minds being closed because we become numb to the desires of others to explore what they believe. And it turns them in the opposite direction because the person doing the shouting is too busy moving their lips than exercising their judgment.

<u>HOPE</u>

Have the Trumpets Blown?

Gospel – Mark 1:1 – 8

References – 2nd Kings 1:8; Psalm 60, 108; Joel 2:12

There once was a king that possessed a very large and ancient relic that was in the shape of an oval with a very small mirror hanging in the middle. The king valued this relic so much so that it was always in the room with him where ever he was or went. He would have his servants carry it from one room and to another.

The order was that it was to never leave his side. No one knew why the king had this affinity for the relic and they never dared ask him because they feared that he would object in a not so positive manner.

But there was a visitor to the kingdom, one day, who just had to know. So he asked the king why he always had to have that oval shaped relic with him at all times.

The king replied that he used this to focus his vision when he had difficult decisions to make. On the opposite side of this oval, he would always have a vision of the two sides to the quandary and this allowed him to blot out all other distractions.

He told the visitor that if one looked hard enough and long enough, with the right framing, through the oval at the mirror, one's eye sight would blend together to see which would be the right decision to make in the end.

The visitor told him that what he was actually seeing was himself and a reflection of how he hoped his decisions would turn out. He was seeing himself as to how he wished he was.

The visitor went on to tell him that if he had prepared his path with the truth then he wouldn't need a mirror to view what has already happened in the past but a clear glass to see what was truly possible out in front.

****

The first line, in the first chapter, in the first Gospel, in the bible says it all, "The beginning of the Gospel of Jesus Christ, the Son of God." Gospel is defined as a proclamation or the Good News and it signals the end of an old relationship and the beginning of a new one between God, the Father, Jesus the Christ, and us.

This one line spells out the whole future plan that God started with Adam and Eve, tried to fix with the flood, attempted to spell out to us broken humans through the prophets, and had to sacrifice His only Son our Lord up there on the cross to show everyone living that Satan does not have ultimate authority over what He created.

You see, Jesus is the new message set apart from the rules and regulations laid down by our Jewish forbearers. For many, this discovery opens the doors in their eyes and hearts to the many possibilities that our Savior has given to us.

It should also give us pause to consider what the Jewish people were doing too. Why they wanted a ruler so bad. Why many of the leaders just couldn't accept what they had spent their entire lifetimes learning. How they could turn inward when the real Messiah came to instruct them to begin looking outward.

Jesus fulfilled over 300 prophecies. Just the notion that Jesus would be born in Bethlehem, told 700 years before it occurred, has a statistical chance of being fulfilled at 1 in 1 million. Daniel proclaimed 500 years before Christ, that this Messiah would appear which had a chance of 1 in 1 million. And Zechariah told how Judas would betray Christ 500 years earlier too. Those chances comes in at 1 in 1 trillion.

History shows that John baptized hundreds of people. They came out in droves to get what he was offering. To get just a little bit of relief from the constant threats that they'll never measure up or that they've been inflicted with the sins of their fathers that had their hearts being hardened by all the rulers of their day.

They stood there and listened. Listened with open ears and open hearts to the Gospel. The Good News. The proclamation that our Savior is coming. And then they prepared themselves for that event.

You know, we can live our whole lives in anticipation of the Eschatology, the end times. We can live out our days in fear that something out there, that we can't even see, will come in and swoop down on us and snuff us out. But, you see, nothing in this world can stop our God the Father from carrying out His will. He is the one in control.

Some will, evidently, have questions about what all this means when taken into consideration all that's going on in our world. Some will choose to walk away, too comfortable with the world they've created for themselves and because someone, somewhere, has told them there ain't no God.

But, folks, anyone who can ignore the facts of history and the facts behind Jesus and all that occurred to get to this point have already determined themselves to be God. Just a God that they have decidedly fits with their own desires. That's sort of what Adam and Even did and the Israelites did and what many have done throughout history.

The king, in our parable, was looking for something that would give him answers to outside questions when all he was really doing was looking at, or within, himself. And when he realized that he was looking within all this time, then he was able to see the truth of what his heart was telling him was the right decision all along. We've been given the Good News all along too.

The parable illustrates that our futures are, as yet, uncharted. We don't even know if we will have a tomorrow. Always looking to the past in our desire or quest to shape the future can be a self-defeating act because the past does not predict the future but only provides lessons to educate us on our futures. What we decide, if we get a future, ourselves will determine that future we want.

<u>HOPE</u>

Just Do It

Gospel – Mark 1:1 – 15

References – Isaiah 42:1; Matthew 28:19

There once was a well-known speaker. This man would travel throughout the land speaking about things that were happening to the people. Much of the time, what he spoke about went directly against the rulers of the day. And this put them on edge. For as many times as that they would discount the man's words, the truth of what he had to say would seem to come about.

Then one day, the rulers decided to jail the man in hopes that it would quiet him. Unfortunately, for them, his words, while in jail, got out and began to have more meaning and purpose. More truth because what he spoke about was now on display for everyone to see for themselves.

The rulers released the man but sent him far away into the desert. They hoped his isolation would calm the people and they would forget what truths the speaker told. However, the speaker continued because many would go and seek him out and return with what he had said.

It seemed that the more the rulers tried to silence the speaker, the more the truth of what he spoke resonated with the people and the rulers then had to deal with even more unrest.

Finally, the people rose up against the rulers because many saw that what the speaker said had merit and was the real truth and he was returned to civilization where, at least, some of the truths he always spoke about were eventually acted upon but everyone living ended up benefitting because the ideas and truths reached to the depths of all including those rulers.

****

Jesus getting baptized. Must've been quite the sight. The crowds would've gathered all around Him and pointed at Him and whispered about Him. The throngs of people surrounding Him must've caused quite the stir too.

Except, no one knew who He was. No one understood who He was. No one, including John the Baptist, realized or truly believed that this Jesus was the true Messiah. All those people that were standing right next to Jesus who had no clue.

Imagine if they knew the real truth and actually believed. What if they knew that this guy was Jesus, the Messiah, and then they could've asked Him questions that we all might want answers to. What if they knew that this guy was Jesus, the Messiah, and then they could've asked for a possible miracle or two?

And then there's the question of why Jesus got baptized in the first place too. He didn't have any sins to forgive. He didn't have to be dead to sin and alive to Christ. He didn't have to do it to get saved or for salvation. He didn't have any congregation to join. He didn't have to get this done in order to participate in His Last Supper, the Eucharist.

But many people are just convinced that the baptism of Jesus was done just one way even though there's no evidence of the method. Some read into it what they want and close off any competing theology. They miss that the purpose of the baptism has never been the method or the legalism that goes with it but the act itself in the command of God, the Father.

You see, Jesus got baptized because that's what His Father told Him to do. Just go do it. God may not have told Jesus to do it in those words but we do get a sense that that's what He said because Mark writes, "and a voice came out of the heavens: 'Thou art My beloved Son, in Thee I am well-pleased.'"

So, there are many reason why we do this baptism thing the way we do it. At the top of the list is the commandment of God, the Father, to just do it. Just go and do it. Since baptism is one of the two pillars of the church worldwide, the other being communion, it's determined to be a gift. It's one of the two for two good reasons. One, because it's what Jesus did and what He commands us to do.

And two because it's a gift from God. A sacrament. A mystery. That's the meaning of sacrament. A mystery. And if you gotta do anything to receive a gift then it's not a gift. And if it's not a gift then you can earn it. And if you can earn it then you don't need Jesus. You can get to heaven on your own. This single point in all of Christendom is the core reason that we can baptize children because they certainly can't do anything to get to heaven on their own and God knows that.

Hence, He gave this mystery as a gift to you and me to show dramatically that you and me are too broken to get there on our own. So, baptism is not an act that you have to know anything about. God has already got It all figured out and all that He says is to do it. To just do it.

So, you say, I'm already baptized. What in the world does this have to do with me? You see, baptism, or baptizmo in the Greek, is the act of washing. It's the act of dipping your hands in the water, giving thanks and remembering your own baptism. It's the act of you standing there in the shower or sitting there in the tub with the water running all over you and remembering you are a child of God.

Now, if you say that just sticking your hands under the water and remembering the life giving grace and mercy that God gives to you is too easy, too little, too minimal, then you're heading into the sphere of works righteousness because you're saying that the gift that God has given you must not be worth very much and you gotta add a little to sweeten the pot.

So, the real questions remain, do you stand in opposition to God by action or inaction? Or do you take this passage and the many others that are written for you and use that as your shield against everything that's telling you that you gotta do something to get this gift from God?

The parable illustrates that regardless of what the world around you wants you to be convinced of, the truth always has a way of poking itself out of the ground the world has tried to drive it into and yelling out for all to hear and those that will listen come to know it for what it is.

Folks, the truth can be locked way but it's really great at picking that lock. The truth can be shoved to the back burner but it has a way of flaming up the senses of those who can smell it for the truth it is. The truth always wins out because it's composed of the light and the light always shine brightly.

<u>HOPE</u>

Ordinary to the Extraordinary

Gospel – Mark 1:9 – 20

References – John 6; 1st Kings 19:19 – 21

There once was a great chef who everyone vied to work for and had a reputation for very unusual meals that were always fawned over and exquisite in taste. When asked, by reporters, about how he could create such masterpieces, the chef told them that every meal starts from scratch but all people see is the final result.

He then took the reporters back to his kitchen and introduced them to the workers and showed them all the initial ingredients. He pointed out that even though each individual item, by itself, does nothing to contribute to the overall dish that comes out of the oven, it is with the combination of each of the items and the team work of the workers that the dish becomes something memorable and a delight.

On one table might be a tomato and an onion and some lettuce as well as other items. Apart, they are OK but put together they make a salad that everyone talks about and wants more of. So it is with the people in the kitchen. Alone, they are just ordinary people all going about their jobs but put together, they combine their talents to produce a meal that everyone will talk about too.

So it is with you and me. Alone, we are limited to ourselves. Together, we can change the world.

****

So, imagine if some total stranger came up to you and said, "Drop everything you're doing and follow me." Imagine if you're just finishing your day, walking out to your car to go home and this guy comes up to you and tells you to follow him and he will make you preachers or apostles or fishers of men or anything else. Or even you've just come from a great day of fishing and this happened. Just imagine. What would you do?

And, this guy says to do it now. Many that went to Him, He turned away and many who were with Him walked away themselves. John 6 speaks of many who said it was just too hard. Just too much of a commitment. Luke and Mark write of over 70 doing just this. Walking away.

You know, we read these passages and I'd bet that none of us have put ourselves in their place. Leaving our jobs. Our livelihoods. Our families. To go off into some unknown to do unknown things with unknown people. But that's just what these guys did. They left everything.

And they suffered for it. Almost all of the disciples met with death. With beatings. With betrayal. Almost all of them, that answered the call of Jesus, put it out there so that you and me could sit here this morning and see that the truth of what Jesus spoke about holds up even under the most stressful of times.

But you might wonder to yourself, how would I respond to that calling? I can tell you that God has got it all figured out and His ideas cannot be broken. I can also tell you that God does not send you alone. He sends support. We may just not see it but that has more to do with our own limited visions and capacity to understand than it does with God's desire for each of us.

Folks, we need to remember that sometimes there are solutions to our problems that we just can't see. That's why we need others. That's why we need the church. That's why we need to pray. Jesus called those first disciples in pairs.

Touched them in a place that they hadn't been touched before and everything within them was grabbing ahold of those words, "Follow Me", and clamoring to move each of their footsteps a little bit closer to the one Savior.

Jesus is here to help you to become something you've never even thought about. He's here to speak to you about being an extraordinary disciple in ways that you couldn't even imagine.

Folks, now is our chance to become something more than what we are or have been. It's our chance to move from the ordinary to the extraordinary but we can only do that through the acceptance of Jesus as the Christ and latch onto that to know that our futures are wrapped up in the propagation of His truth and Good News.

Folks, now's the time to take ahold of the person sitting next to you, living next to you, is in line at the grocery store in front of you and hold on because Jesus has said that He's coming back and to be prepared. Part of that is to try and make sure that all those you love and all those you know are ready and prepared too.

The parable illustrates that even you can turn into the extraordinary just as the chef made the cake from simple ingredients with the help of others. Just as the chef turned ordinary parts of everyday items into something to be marveled at.

Let yourself be changed into something that's good to the eyes and ears of our Savior by letting go of what this world wants to convince you of and hang on to the truth of what our Savior has shown as the real facts. You can choose to follow this world with its broken promises or the heaven that's never ending and will always bring truth. Turn from the ordinary to the extraordinary.

<u>HOPE</u>

The Pain in Being Truthfully Honest

Gospel – Luke 2:21 – 40

References – Isaiah 8:14; Ezekiel 14:17

Years ago, there were these two young men. They were your average guys that did whatever teens do. But they were in the wrong place at the wrong time. They got caught up in a sting and ended up doing a combined 45 years, added together, for a murder they didn't commit. They even confessed to the murder.

Now, the two confessions didn't match but that wasn't important. They confessed never the less. Truth flew out the window those 30 years ago. Honesty on the part of the convicted men as well as those who forced the confession hid beneath the evil that is always lurking. They served time for something they did not do while the one who did the actual crime walked free. To this date, that person has still not been found and probably never will.

Why would someone confess to something they didn't do? It happens all too frequently. The frailty of the human condition is such that we're never as strong as we like to think we are.

The point of this is that without a firmer hand from God, we can cross over a line that we don't even recognize most of the time. After we have crossed over, we always hope that we can walk it back at some point in the future. Without God and Jesus, our futures are closed to that possibility.

With Jesus, all things are still possible. Through Jesus, even these two men, who are now free, can begin again.

****

You know, it can be trying, at times, but there are always two sides of the same coin and no matter how you flip that coin of life, it will always be a guess as to which side it will land on. In other words, the blessings and the problems you come into any season of life with will be the same ones you take out. The difference will be what you do with those blessings and problems or what do those do with you and to you.

One is where your attention is on yourself rather than those of the people around you. Your concerns will then seem to be overwhelming because you are alone. The second is where your attention is on those around you. That enables you to focus on others and while your own issues will not go away, they do seem to diminish a bit.

Jesus came into this world as a pauper. His pop didn't even have enough money to buy a lamb so two doves were selected when they went to the temple. The choice of the lower class. Yea, Jesus was not from the upper class but His work was on the highest order. He was sent here by God, the Father, in order that you can stand before Him blameless. You see, it's how we look at where we are all at that determines where we will be.

Now, many look around them and are inundated with news on either the media or our computers. We get tunnel vision and then our own futures are uncertain. This world has had centuries to tell us that everything is hopeless and we should just chuck it all in and give up. This world has told us, through our leaders, that it has the solution to all our problems.

Now, they say that honesty is the best policy. While that may be true, speaking that honesty can lead us into troubled waters especially if the conditions in which we live are rife with making sure that everyone is happy. In our current cancel culture climate, honesty is turned into narrative and speaking the truth, the real truth, is viewed as bigoted or some other catch phrase. Because, that honesty, that truth is going to rub some people raw. If Simeon had been around today, I'd venture to guess that he'd be canceled.

Simeon said that this child, Jesus, was destined for the falling and rising of many in Israel. Simeon was telling the painful truth of the matter to all who were listening and many who didn't want to know. Simeon was telling all those people listening that what they have become is a direct reflection on what they believe. So, Simeon would definitely be fact checked in our social media norms of today.

Fortunately for us, Jesus really didn't care if those that wanted to turn His message of Good News into equal opportunity for all really rejected the message all together. Jesus only cared that the people of His time heard the unmitigated truth and what they did with it was up to them. The truth of Jesus is rarely affected by feelings.

Simeon spoke it like it was and Jesus was, and is, brought into our world each and every year to reinforce the ideas that you and I can begin to live out the promises that God, the Father, gave to us.

The birth of Jesus was not just about a small child that was conceived by the Holy Spirit being born in a stable out in the middle of nowhere. It's about a rebirth of all of us that can allow us to live out our calling in justified grace and mercy. Jesus came to us to pierce His sword in our side just like a sword was pierced in His up on that cross.

The parable illustrates that while we are weak in our brokenness, we have the strength of truth at our backs to show us that possibilities exist for our futures. Whatever futures that God deems we will have. The two men that were imprisoned still have possibilities with their lives because Jesus came down here from God to give them and us that possibility. All things are possible with Jesus.

<u>HOPE</u>

To All the Lowly

Gospel – Mark 1:1 – 8

References – Psalm 87:6; Isaiah 1:3; Acts 5

For years, a small town prided itself on building ships. This was a small coastal town in Maryland that was made up of peaceful people who just wanted to live out their lives in coexistence with all the other towns surrounding them. Their character was for building powerful schooners and that reputation spanned the many shores in the country.

But soon, war came and the town had to come up with a method of keeping from being destroyed by the invading navy and army. The town's people were all evacuated and all were distraught at the idea that they would have nothing to come back to.

But there was a bright young man who came up with a method of fooling the enemy in their attack. His job was nightly carrying around the lamps that lit the streets and he got the idea to put the lamps high in trees so that the gun boats off shore would fire into the air, thus missing the town altogether.

This "blackout" was successful with the exception of one home that was hit and is known as the Cannonball house to this day. Since the war of 1812, some say this story was just legend but the town has existed to this day.

The gist is that what's seen and talked about and written about may not be historically accurate but it's in the retelling and underlying points that the real truths may come to be known and held dear.

****

Luke has, probably, the best story of the birth of our Savior than any of the Gospels in the bible. Neither Mark nor John has a birth narrative and Matthew approaches it from a completely different point of view with different ancillary players – the wise men. My guess is that it all depends on context.

It's also noteworthy that the timeline, in Luke, doesn't match with any historical analysis of what was really going on back then. The census wouldn't have been done by Augustus but by Quirinius as referenced in Acts, Chapter 5 and the Roman regulation of having to return to the place of origin just didn't exist.

But, Luke approaches literally everything from what the coming of the Messiah means to the world and to the history of the world. What it means for you and me. What it redefines in our relationship to the Father. What it fulfills in terms of prophecy so that we can all have assurances that His coming has happened. From the very onset of this chapter, Luke attributes the whole episode in relation to God and us.

In verse 7, "And she gave birth to her first-born son; and she wrapped Him in cloths, and laid Him in a manger, because there was no room for them in the inn." There's 4 major parts to this that many will just overlook but these 4 parts are key as to why Luke wrote what he did and why this birth is tantamount to a full understanding of why Jesus coming here to save you and me is integral to what we believe.

The 1st part is the "And she gave birth to her first-born son." Folks, that tells us that Jesus was with God in the beginning. Before time. Before everything and anything else. Sitting there at God's right hand. Seeing all that He has planned. In ancient times, the first born of a family would inherit the estate. Inherit the blessings. Inherit the benefits as well as the adversity that was created by their father.

The 2nd part is the "and she wrapped Him in cloths." It was Jewish custom to tightly wrap a new baby in linen so that their limbs would grow straight. Less breakage. And this also is to show us that we should keep on the straight and narrow too, as they say. Keep our eyes firmly transfixed on heaven directly because He will be returning. Any time. Any day.

The 3rd part is the "and laid Him in a manger." The manger that probably existed was a feeding trough. It could've also been a stall. The manger is mentioned 3 times, closely together, so we should pay attention to how important that manger really was in Luke's eyes. We have no information as to what it really was. The manger is another way of allowing that Jesus was there to feed the world.

And finally, the 4th part which says, "Because there was no room for them in the inn." I believe Luke was showing that there was no room at the inn because he wanted to show that Jesus went against the normal view of the day. Didn't go with the crowd so to speak. Led rather than followed. Made His own path ours to follow.

The final thoughts are that we can take from the birth of our Savior that idea that we too can begin anew. We too can be born of light and thus be able to snuff out the darkness. Jesus bring promises. Jesus shows us that no matter what we have gone through that there's possibility waiting.

The parable illustrates that our own stories and histories can be shared even after we're gone and those that follow can learn from them and allow them to bring fullness to everyone's lives. Our legacy is not what we do in the here and now but the stories we've left behind. The small town that had humble beginnings shows that even when we do not recognize our contributions, others, after us, can grab those contributions by us and use them raise everyone's boats.

HUMILITY

Absolute Power

Gospel – Mark 6:14 – 29
References – 1st Kings 21; Romans 3

There once was a man who always thought he was right. It really didn't matter the outcome of any action or event, he would always frame it so that he could convince, at least himself, that he was right. Even those things that went wrong on a grand scale, this man was right.

Everyone around him knew the opposite though. They looked at him as a blow hard because they knew that with such an attitude, no responsibility accompanied this guy's thoughts and, therefore, no learning or growing.

But, one day, the man made a mistake on such a scale that those around him just knew he would have to take responsibility for it. But, to their dismay, he didn't. He didn't live up to his actions and that resulted in everyone around him suffering. So they left him alone. All alone.

And the man would end his days completely alone with himself because his own house all around him had virtually crumbled. Without others in our lives, we can show no real responsibility because our own definition of responsibility is what we have determined to be right. And that would be broken because we are broken.

****

This Gospel section is where Herod is remembering when and why he had John beheaded. Herod was what was called a tetrarch, or sub-king of Galilee under Roman rule. He was known as Herod Antipas but Herod for short.

Herod just couldn't wait for his brother to die, so he took his brother's household, his wife more specifically, all because, as the scripture says, he was beguiled and she was power hungry. The traditions written about this differ somewhat but the essence of the story remains the same even with non-Christian authors such a Josephus.

The point of knowing this story is that it illustrates that with power comes responsibility. With humbleness, kindness. With power comes a duty for fairness. With humbleness, fairness with humility. With power comes a willingness to learn. With humbleness, learning to be taught.

So, what does this scripture have to do with you and me? It illustrates our own constant desire to be God. To build our own tower of Babel's. To define what is, ultimately, right and wrong from our own perspectives.

To compare ourselves with others around us and look on their outside rather than what's on the inside, the part that God has implanted in all of us. To look without really seeing the beauty of another without detecting the person beneath.

Now, I'm not saying that we consciously want to be God but, rather, we go about our days making decisions based on our gut instinct or our relative instruction. We wake up in the morning not with the renewed vigor of someone who has escaped death one more time but with the view that our problems determine our future.

Josephus, writes that "The destruction of Herod's army seemed to be divine vengeance, and certainly a just vengeance, for his treatment of John." I believe this Gospel is illustrating the most human tendency we all have which is that our own attempts to define right from wrong outside the confines of scripture or logic sooner or later come back to our own doorsteps but our courage to accept that error falters.

You see, Herod could have changed his mind. Could have rescinded his order and honored his friend, John. He could have told his wife and daughter no and had his daughter request something else. But pride reared its ugly head. Pride got in the way.

This Gospel illustrates that the decisions we make can be and are influenced by what's going on around us and the pushes and pulls of those wanting us to move this way or that. This Gospel tells us that we should sometimes take that breath and rethink of what it is that Jesus would have us do in those moments when the sounds of the world are crashing into us to get us to move its way.

The parable illustrates that when we do not have humility, when we do not accountability to ourselves from our self, when we ignore the realty of our actions then we're exhibiting a self-perpetuating narcissism. The man who always thought he was right was wrong simply because the logic of always being right is fallacious. So it is with rulers, dictators, elected officials, and us.

HUMILITY

Humility

Gospel – Mark 7:24 – 37

There once was a young man who grew up watching all those politicians on the news and decided that doing that was what he wanted to do. He ran for student council President when he was in high school and won. He ran for council President when he was in college and won. He even ran for a seat on his county board and won. Every time, it seemed, that this man ran for an office, he would win.

And when he won he served his term with honor and dignity. Always putting the people he represented first and doing what he said on the campaign trail he would do. Even those who voted against him or ran against him had respect for him because this man did what he promised and really looked out for his people.

Then the man ran for a seat in US House of Representatives and won. But when he got to Washington, he was met by several senior members and they put pressure on the guy to do what was in their own self-interest.

At first he refused but, as time went by, he relented. At the first it was on small things but then a matter came up that, if he had voted for the bill, it would have harmed his people but it would have enriched the man and his colleagues. If he voted against the bill it would have cost not only himself and all his colleagues but would have benefitted the people.

He voted for the bill but he lost the next election. Our morals are always on the line whether we know it or not. How we approach each decision determines where our tomorrows will take us. Jesus says to choose wisely.

****

I've read this passage from Mark literally 100's of times and each time I keep coming back to the words, "Sir, even the dogs under the table eat the children's crumbs." But that's the least of it because of the preceding verse, "Let the children be fed first, for it is not fair to take the children's food and throw it to the dogs." This shows Jesus in a very bad light for rejecting Gentiles.

Well, to fully understand this interaction one must look at how they referred to each other in those days. Jews generally referred to Gentiles as dogs. That's right. As dogs. The Gentiles were not the chosen people.

But Jesus cut through this – albeit without some push back. He was bested by this Syrophoenician woman and, as a result, her child was cured of evil spirits. What this interchange speaks about mostly, is humility. This kind of humility that allows another's opinion to be right. Seems we have seen a lot of "UN"humility as of late but Jesus shows us that real humility is relooking at what one says and taking the course that it requires.

Humility. It comes in many shapes and sizes and, in this Gospel, can be simultaneous. The woman has to have some level of humility to go to Jesus to begin with and Jesus has to return that humility by recognizing the woman's point and then acting on it. Humility comes from the Latin word for "humus" which means "of the earth" Now, coincidentally, Adam means the same thing. Of the earth.

But Jesus shows us what humility is. He spars with the woman and allows her logic and pleas to shine through. He looks at her in a light that says that yes, she is a person worthy of grace and mercy. Not what the Jews have already decided she was. Worthy to have her troubles taken care of. Worthy to be listened to.

Our lives are lived out by our own expectations. We generally wake up each day expecting that what came before will probably be what lays ahead. Our own sense of self generally takes over and we walk by, drive by, and pass by those that reach out to us in ways that are not readily apparent. Our lives are spent in our own sense of worth rather than in the humility of the one who gave us our very own grace and mercy.

Keeping in mind that what a person wants is usually hidden underneath their exterior guarded by their pride. Our real challenge is to ask from Jesus what this woman asked in the humility that she approached Him with and then spread that gift of healing to all those we come into contact with.

The parable illustrates how we can be manipulated by the avarice of this world and that when we put others first then we will benefit because we've put aside our own self-aggrandizement for the benefit of the people of God. The man gave up his principles for his own self-enrichment. He may have won in the short term but he lost the war. The parable illustrates that truth always wins in the end even it takes longer than we want it to. Even those whom we think are untouchable are always judged by their actions by the Father or all Fathers who see and hear all.

<u>IDENTITY</u>

Family

Gospel – Mark 3:19 – 35

References – Matthew 28:19; Ephesians 2

One day, little Adam was walking home from school. As he passed by the old sandlot, there was a group of older, bigger kids there that always picked on him. This day was no different. So Adam took out running.

He found himself in another part of his neighborhood that had kids his age but were not of his background so he really didn't have anything to do with them. His family used to caution him about going into that neighborhood because the people there were low class. But when Adam entered into this neighborhood he was greeted by some kids his own age who welcomed him to play a little baseball.

Soon Adam became great friends and he found out that each of these new kids had made a pact with each other to watch their backs because the older, bigger kids were always picking on them due to where they lived.

Adam soon found out that this pack helped him when he would encounter the bigger kids because the bigger kids wouldn't bother him when he had his new friends around since the reality was the bigger kids were kind of afraid of these other kids.

Adam had found himself a new family that supported him when times got tough and rejoiced with him when time were good. It's our desire to be liked and accepted that helps to drive our lives to become a part of a family that lifts us up in ways that we can shine. Jesus called us all to be a family of faithful so that each of us can carry out the grace and mercy of the Father to those who are searching.

****

Families. They are people composed of unexpected responses to desired questions. Families usually come with the biggest surprises and definitely unexpected expectations. You see, they are organizations that do not fit any classical structure because, quite simply, they're all different.

In this Gospel, Jesus upsets the family structure. He has invited those who are followers and believers into the family of God while those on the outside just don't have eyes to see nor ears to hear.

In this way, Jesus simultaneously brings into a new family all those who've been cast out by their earthly families by following Jesus and has created a new sense of belonging that could only come from God.

It's hard for many in today's times too. From those that are persecuted and even put to death for converting from Islam to Christianity overseas to the person that has denied the agnostic teachings of their parents to accept the life that brings a certain hope and joy of believing in the Christ, it happens with regularity and it never happens in a vacuum.

Jesus is not denying his own mother and brothers in this Gospel despite the way it sounds. After all, it's His brother James that's the leader of the Christian Jerusalem community.

I see churches that exclude people simply by absence rather than direct welcoming. Those that walk into our sanctuary are all looking for the grace that we are commissioned by God and the Holy Spirit to give. There are too many churches that split due to earthly passions that deny the mission of the church itself.

The church is a sanctuary for those with heavy hearts and those who've lost their way. It's a building yes, but much,

much more. It can be a place where all are welcomed or welcomed back.

The parable illustrates what we consider our families. Is it those that we are necessarily born with or those that lift us up? Is our families those who we grew up with or those that grew with us in our own life's journeys? Is our families those that stand beside us without looking at who we are or are they those that stand at our back ready to look out for us in places we cannot see or detect? Jesus illustrated what a family was.

<u>IDENTITY</u>

Seeking Our True Identity

Gospel – John 8:31 – 38

References – Romans 8:20 – 21; Galatians 5:1

There once was a young boy who was adopted at an early age. Throughout his life, his adoptive parents would tell him this fact but they would never tell him anything about his natural parents.

So, when the young boy, who was a young man now, turned 18 he decided that he would seek out the history of himself. His adoptive parents told him to go ahead but to please never forget who raised him to be the person he was. So the young man set out.

Along the way, he ran across another much older man who told him that who he began as does not determine who he will be. Who he was raised by and their values and truth has a much greater impact on what he will be. And who he has listened to will directly affect where he will find himself later on in life.

If he can listen to the underlying truths that are the basis for all the surface emotions, if he can remember the values that were instilled in him growing up, if he can remember the presence of his adoptive parents and what they stood for, he will find that his future can be one that shows the real certainties in his life.

With that, the young man decided that he had found the truth to his personage and turned and went back home.

****

The question of who am I most certainly morphs into the question of who is God. We are created in His image and who we believe we are and what we believe about ourselves ultimately revolves around who we believe God is and what we believe about God. And, by relation, Jesus the Christ.

The Gospel is as much about what the Jews thought then as it is about what we think and, more importantly, portray today. You see, we're all enslaved just as the Jews were even during the time of Christ.

But, sometimes, our own enslavement is not apparent to us. It's not only until we take a good hard look at where we are, who we listen to, what we say, what we write, that we can begin to see all the little things we've become comfortable with to just simply accepting.

We're enslaved by expectations of family, bosses, even governments. We're enslaved by what we project to the public. We're enslaved by our own visions of who we are. Just like the Jews of Jesus' day. They were enslaved by their Roman rulers. They just deluded themselves into self-believing that they were free.

The Jews of Jesus' day were enslaved by the myriad of regulations put in place not only by their Roman captors but by the very people who were supposed to know better, the Pharisees and elders and Sadducees. The myriad of regulations that were designed to tax them to the point of never ending servitude and to control them through edicts and derived laws. Sound familiar?

When you buy a piece of land or a house. Save and scrimp for that homestead. Work until you're 60 or 70 to pay it off. The government is there with their hand out because of property taxes. Because of regulations. So, who really owns that land? Who controls it?

When you work most of your adult life and put money into a government run savings account to pay you back after you retire but then find out that the very government that said it was your savings account reclassifies it to be a benefit to be doled out by them since they spent all your savings, who is really the slave? Isn't that savings plan just another tax we're obligated to pay by the master? Are we really free?

When you go to buy that gasoline that you need in your vehicle because, without it, you can't get to work and you end up paying over 30 to 50 percent of the cost in hidden government enacted taxes, are you any different from the Jews even in the days when they were slaves building the pyramids in Egypt?

But, folks, Jesus was telling those Jews then and He's telling you and me today that our future is not of this world in the here and now. He's saying that when we can look our own realities in the face and come to the conclusion that Jesus is the one that brings the truth and the reality to light it's only then that we can even start to see our own lives for what they really are.

That we are broken but with the promises of the grace and mercy and, quite frankly, the forgetfulness of God because of the promise that Jesus will stand right beside us when we have to stand before the throne, then and only then can we look at all that's around us and come to the forgone conclusion that this world is not the ultimate goal.

In Jesus' day it took close to another 30 years for those Jews to revolt. But the people of Luther's day saw that they could be free. We had a movement ourselves around 200 years ago too but the people of today seemed to be swayed more from the 10 second sound bite than real truth.

Have memories that last all of 10 minutes and then it's on to the next YouTube or Facebook video. Something more exciting. Develop opinions that are based on feelings rather than hard evidence. And we are seeing a whole generation that repeats to itself, "We have never yet been enslaved to anyone."

The freedom that you and I enjoy is not given by any other human being on this planet but by the grace and mercy of God almighty and only by Him. For we're not truly free because we're looking downward but we can be free once and for all if we look upward.

Jesus said, to be free is to find that place where you can answer what and who you are. Jesus said, to be free is to recognize the realities of your current station in life and then to reach out to someone who can set you free from those chains.

Jesus said, our thinking must rise above the day to day machinations of those seeking to hold us down and rise to the occasion of being the disciples we were created to be.

The parable illustrates a simple question, "How could a flawed opinion coming from a flawed person or flawed media be anything other than flawed?" When we claim a history but reject a future then we're like the young man in our parable. He wanted to find his future by seeking out his history. But no matter what that young man might have found it's only what the older man told him that made the most sense. That who we become is not necessarily where we have come from but on what we will rely on to make us what we were designed to be.

<u>JUDGING</u>

Inside vs. Outward Knowledge

Gospel – Matthew 6:1 – 6, 16 – 21
References – 2nd Corinthians 4:18

There once was a very famous actor. This guy would play comedies and serious roles too. He got his start in the business by playing someone who was lost from another planet that landed in a small town. The role grew and he was marked by it in ways that ran deep into his heart.

He was considered one of this countries legends but his life on the outside didn't match what he hid from others on the inside. He was tormented by hidden demons that only he could see. He soon could not bear it out and he ended up taking his own life.

The point of this is that there was no indication that this guy actually believed in anything other than himself. And when doubt creeped in, which it always does, this actor could no longer act a part that made fantasy become reality and he viewed his life as nothing but a shell game.

He didn't have an overriding belief in anything other than what he could touch and see. And that will always leave one with a deep sense of emptiness.

****

This Gospel is about what we live inside versus how we live on the outside. It's about the value we put on what we do rather than what we believe. It's about living a life that is vacuous of real meaning to our souls while trying to substitute the essence of what is good for our own ideals. The reality of what's on your inside versus the picture we paint of what we want the world to see. Sometimes, those two are close but they're almost never the same long term.

When we take the ashes of Ash Wednesday, we're acknowledging that Jesus came for us and died for us. We're visibly taking a mark that says we are children of God. We're being reminded that we really are nothing to this world but everything to our Savior. We're knowing that from ashes we came and to ashes we will return. That there will be very little of what we do during our short time on this earth that will forever last except the memories that we create for those left behind.

The ashes that are put on our foreheads can be a calling for us to affect people around us. It's a symbol but that symbol tells yourself, most of all, that the amazing grace of our Lord will always be in our head if we can listen. We're here for a very short time. What we leave behind is a testament to what we live for every day.

Each of us has the choice to be remembered. Or not. Each of us has the opportunity to have what we leave to those left behind, a legacy of Jesus or a blank slate. As you come to have the celebration of Jesus' triumphant entry into Jerusalem and His legacy of belief in eternal life spread on your forehead, what is your selection?

The parable illustrates that it really doesn't matter what we portray to others, what we believe about ourselves rules over the façade of illusion we pretend to be. What people see is not necessarily what we are and what we are will always win out because it's what on that inside that controls our outward directions in the end.

LAW

Common Sense

Gospel – Mark 2:23 – 3:6

There once was set of parents that were very strict towards all their children. Not in the sense that the children shouldn't lie or cheat or steal but in more minute ways that covered things like what they were to wear or which toys they were to play with or even what foods they were to eat.

Now, on the surface, couldn't we all agree that children need some guidance as to what is proper or not? But the parents took this to the extreme even to the point of counting out the number of peas on the plate and even the number of corn niblets. Surely things that would seem excessive.

But, one day, the patriarch of the family arrived for a visit and when she sat down at the dinner table and was served, she shook her head. When she could only sit on the couch with an even number of pillows on it, she just closed her eyes in wonderment. When she had to go to the bathroom and could only use the laid out towels to dry her hands she finally had had enough.

She confronted the parents and told them that they had missed the mark and, as a result, resentment had grown in their children. Resentment that would eventually drive those very children away. Never to return.

The same can be said of us within our churches and how the churches operate and how we operate with each other.

****

Law and tradition. Law and Gospel. It seems to me that law and tradition are one and the same while law and Gospel are diametrically opposed. But we sometimes revert to what the Pharisees did when confronted by a notion that was new and non-traditional.

We retreat into our security of good order to dispute what is new or what is not understood by the history and traditions of our faith. We sometimes revert to the age old mantra of that's not how we did it back then. And we sometimes use the mantra of it not being how our forefathers in the faith or church did it.

Jesus was describing, to those in power, where they missed the mark. He wasn't there to discount all the laws and traditions, just those that perverted the truest meanings of what God set down. Love the Lord your God with all your heart, with all your soul, and with all your mind. And love your neighbor as yourself.

Jesus was going against this good order proscribed by the Pharisees and posting His good news up on the proverbial doors of the Temple just as Luther did in Wittenberg. Jesus had it right, for sure, when He stated that the Sabbath was for us and that we are not for the Sabbath. The laws are for man not the reverse. Not man is made for the law.

When something is introduced, it should be measured against what is scriptural and what is logical. The same that Luther did back in his time and what Jesus was trying to get across to the Pharisees of His time.

We have a lot of discontent in today's society about certain laws that are challenged. I hear the phrase that the Supreme Court is the law of the land all the time. That the law is settled. I could substitute the word Pharisees for our present day Supreme Court. The Jews of that time would have said the law is settled, that the Pharisees laws are the laws of the land.

It's a very fine line that we walk in our day to day lives. We are hit left and right in the news of the social movements of the day. Most of these movements would die off an unnatural death if not given the air time that they're given because they are based on the very notion that we simple folks need the rule makers to determine what God has already decreed. These movements seek to cure what is incurable. The sin of humans.

It ignores the basic notion that God and Jesus have already determined that we're all equal. The problem, logically speaking, is that if these movements are successful, then those that have been discriminated against become the very same people that they are fighting against and they become the discriminators they so despise.

Jesus says that all are equal in the eyes of God. That all deserve the grace and mercy given as a gift by God. That no group of people deserve more than another from God. And that no group of people will receive an inordinate share of gifts from God.

Our challenge is not to live by the movement de jure but to live by the movement of time immortal. The movement of Jesus. Our challenge is to spread the good news that promotes Jesus' notions of laws that are not at all restrictive in their use but lifts everyone up.

The parable illustrates that we can get all caught up with defining the rules that we forget the grace. We can get all caught up with not assessing why something is worth holding on to that we can alienate others from joining the idea. We can put upon others, so much so, that those very others will rebel and then we're left with nothing. The parable speaks to our desire for order when it's that order that calls out to our desire to have grace and mercy.

<u>LIGHT</u>

What is Your True Depth?

Gospel – Matthew 4:23 – 5:12

References – Isaiah 61:1 – 11, 40:31

One day, a man was preparing to leave his office in the late afternoon. Now, this man was very successful in his business and serviced many clients. Some were problems and he would have to tell them the truth in not such a direct manner. Others were much more easier going and the man found he didn't have to make up as much to give them the news. But then this man finally left his office for the day.

As he left to make the journey home, he would approach people and he had the strange sensation that he could see right through some of the people even though they appeared normal. He saw their outlines. Others, he would see them only partially and others he saw as one would normally see someone.

As the trip progressed, this happened more and more, so much so, that the man thought he might be going a bit blind. So he went to his eye doctor. But after an exam, his eye doctor told him that there wasn't anything wrong with his sight.

And as he was leaving the doctor's office, once again he would see people in various forms, from solid to partial to completely transparent.

When he got on the bus, he sat next to another person and heard what they were talking about. Nothing but gossip and negativity. Then he looked at that person and they seemed to be one of the ones that appeared transparent.

Then he got off the bus and walked past a homeless man on the streets. Solid. He then glanced down at his own two hands and found that they were also transparent.

****

Blessed are the poor. Blessed are those who mourn. Blessed are the gentle. Blessed are those hunger and thirst. Blessed are the merciful. Blessed are the pure in heart. Blessed are the peacemakers. Blessed are the persecuted. Blessed are the ones who have been lied about. Ever think about all of this? Do you find yourself in one of the categories? The nine categories?

I guess the thing to ask ourselves is, do we feel blessed or do we feel torn down by everything around us? Can we look at even the littlest of blessings, where events happen, where help is needed and see that for what it is? A gift from God.

You know it's not always the big things but all the little things that happen to us that allows us to see and hear things we might not have even considered a blessing.

But, in our Gospel, Jesus talks about people who are currently in one predicament but can be in another. Jesus speaks of these people in the here and now but says their future is promising. He said that about the people in His time and, quite frankly, He's speaking to us today. Remember, our time is not God's time and, as the Son of God, is not Jesus' time either.

Jesus didn't require anything of anyone in order to receive the healing powers of His grace. They didn't have to go get baptized. They didn't have to go join some church or small group. They didn't even have to go on some mission trip to some impoverished areas. They didn't have to do anything except to just show up.

That's what this is all about. Healing. Healing us from all the stuff we get caught up in on a day to day basis that pulls us from the truth of God and the mercy of Jesus the Christ. And then listening. Hearing the promises that are said because Jesus gives 9 of them right here.

But Jesus is here to tell us something different. He says that despite all the setbacks we may encounter on a day to day basis, despite all the news we hear on a day to day basis, despite all that's going on in the world that makes our present look bleak and without hope, our future is those promises that He's given in this passage.

Those healings are for us. We don't have to do anything to get them, just show up. Show up and listen. Show up and be the disciple that this day is for. The disciple that our God, yours and my God, has created us for.

You see, believing is not some philosophy of life. It ain't some card that you carry that says you're in. It ain't even some merit badge that you can use to prove to others that you're a mature Christian. Believing is a concrete way of living so that the leaders of this world can't have a hold on you and direct you for their glory.

The parable illustrates that we can be like the people walking on the streets in our parable. We can even be the people on that bus. And then what happens is we become like the man who realized that he was no different than the people who could be seen completely through. We become without substance or depth.

<u>LOVE</u>

Jesus' Conversations

Gospel – John 17:1 – 19

Every morning, Beth would start her day by praying for her kids. Over time, she included all those in her church. Soon enough, she started to pray for not only those who she knew but even for people she couldn't identify or even lived in her own town.

When others found out about this, they asked her why she did it. It took up most of Beth's morning and the neighbors wondered why she found it important to pray for those people she didn't know and probably would never know.

Beth told them that even if she didn't know the people she was praying for, those people might have an effect on the things they do with the people she did know so she was, in effect, double praying for her neighbors.

Maybe if we as disciples of God would do as Beth does then it's quite possible that the world would be a much nicer and safer place for all.

****

This Gospel speaks of one praying for the safety and guidance of others. It speaks of giving something so others will have abundant life. So they will have God present in their lives.

You see Jesus is doing something He has never done before in any of the previous passages of John – He is speaking directly to God on behalf of those God has given to Him – His disciples.

I have sat with mothers as their babies were sick, some were even dying, and I saw the pain in their faces. I have prayed with mothers in much the same way that Jesus prayed to God that no danger would befall on their children when they left home for college, or for work, or to even go out into the dangers of the world. I have prayed with mothers that God would shield them by the power of His name so that they could be protected and safe.

But our experiences with our own mothers can be challenging too. Regardless of whether your experience is good or bad with your own mother, regardless of the memories that we all have towards our mothers, nature has embedded this protection and acceptance gene within our mothers.

But life is complicated. So are the people closest to us. There are times when it's easy to appreciate our mothers and times when they can just be the darnedest people.

When Jesus is speaking to His father to protect and nurture His disciples, His people, I can't help but relate this to the loving mother that prays every night for their children. I can't help but think about all those women who gave of themselves to lift up their children.

The parable illustrates one person who's looking after another. Prayer is one form of communication that exists between two entities. It is intimate. Personal. When we pray as Jesus did to His father for others, we are emulating Jesus' concern for all those He's in charge of. When we pray for others we take on the role of advocate on their behalf. And just as Beth started out with prayer for those closest to her, her realization of the effect of one person with another led her to include everyone. As we should too.

SALVATION

Identity

Gospel – John 6:35 – 50

References – Proverbs 9:5; Isaiah 54:13; Jeremiah 31:33

There once was a king in a land that was rather small. The king always ruled over his subjects in a manner that gave them confidence that he was just. Everything the king did and the words that he spoke gave truth to the ears of those who came before him so that everyone went away feeling that their position was heard honestly even if they didn't win the day.

But one day, a person came into the kingdom that pulled the king away from his moral duties. This person would whisper into the king's ear to side with the one that made the new person more wealthy. This person had the confidence and total control of the king.

Soon, the subjects of that kingdom revolted. They threw the new person out and killed him. They caused the king to lose his seat on the throne too. The kingdom was in shambles.

But, soon enough a wise man entered the kings life. One that the king respected. The wise man caused the king to discard those ideas of the new person and come back to the seat of justice and truth and to do it in front of those that had overcome him. This the king did and those that were against him forgave him because they knew the king had returned to the position entrusted to him to work for his subjects.

****

The Gospel centers around identity. Who do the people believe Jesus is? Some kid that grew up with them back in the day, or the true Son of God, the redeemer, the justifier, the truth, the Bread of Life.

It's not like they haven't personally witnessed the miracles that Jesus did. It's not that they didn't know their own history and how a Messiah is to come, and it's not like they couldn't see for themselves how He had fulfilled their own prophecy time and time again.

But, you know, most of us go through life on one course when circumstances call to choose another. The real choice we have is whether we take those chances that might just be the start of something that would go beyond our imaginations.

Those people 2,000 plus years ago were faced with a change in circumstances too. To identify with whom they would recognize as their new identity, their new reality. To come to understand that the one to whom they were speaking with was just not some guy from their hometown but was one that would eventually lead them to a new understanding of what God's grace and mercy was all about.

What Jesus was telling the folks then is what He's telling us now. To be relieved of hunger and thirst as Jesus is saying is not ever to be physically hungry or thirsty but be assured that you will never die, inside.

The parable illustrates that we can all get so caught up in our own sense of importance that we lose sight of the effects that our actions can have on those who rely on our vision.

The king listened to the voice of the sweet but was left tasteless for the trials of those he was entrusted with ruling over. We do too. The king was swayed by the easy suggestions of one who had their own interests in mind over the lives of his subjects. We can do the same too. The parable shows that once we can regain the sanity of the truth we can come back to our own spheres of influence in order to raise everyone up for a better future.

<u>SALVATION</u>

Missing the Point

Gospel – John 6:51 – 59

References – Matthew 18:20; Hebrews 10:24

There once was an old sailor who had been at sea most of his life. From an early teenager to his now ripe old age of 70. He visited lands far and wide on his sailing ship. Letting the winds take him where they may.

He wasn't concerned with losing his way because he always knew that his maps of the seas and his compass would always allow him to stay on the right course. Even in the toughest of winds you would find him trimming the sails to take full advantage of what God and nature dished out.

He knew that once he put his compass point on a destination, he would arrive because his compass had never failed him and it was a tool given to him created by workmen who knew the value in getting it right.

Maybe we could point our own lives in much the same manner to keep us from falling overboard in the winds of time or change. Maybe we could have belief in our faith enough that would allow us to chart a course for our lives that would let us enjoy all beauty that God has for us even in our hectic lives. Maybe.

****

You see, this is the 4th Gospel passage that's still talking about what Jesus was trying to get across to those around Him. That He's the New Bread of Life. But they still didn't get it. I wonder if we, sitting here today, truly get it either.

We still have trouble, on most days, understanding that what we have around us is just a small part of the gift that Jesus came back from that empty tomb to lay on us. That our own personal histories are marked by times where we turn away from the one that came back from that empty tomb and is knocking on our doors.

We can so easily overlook the signs that have been laid out for us. It's very human to keep from looking inward to the soul that belongs to Christ and, instead, begin to look outward to the demands of society thereby missing the roads that have already been cleared for us.

The Gospel is speaking about an idea. An idea that's old to the Jews of the time but new in that it also went against everything they had been taught. They questioned the ability of Jesus to offer up His body and His blood as a substitute for their ritual sacrifice.

You see, the Jews, of the time, viewed what Jesus was telling them as going against the very teachings and actions of Moses on all levels. Where they claimed that God sent manna down to them via Moses and here was Jesus saying that, no, God didn't feed you manna from Moses but Jesus was and is the manna, the real Bread of Life. The real manna from Heaven.

Jesus is talking about much more than just a Eucharistic meal. He's talking about a community that comes together and takes His body and His blood and dines on it together as a community. His Eucharistic meal isn't a litmus test on all people everywhere to see if one is worthy or not to be a part of the ecclesia. His Eucharistic meal is an invitation to everyone because they're not perfect, not Holy, not in line with whatever is popular at the moment.

We're all hypocrites simply because we're broken and we need at least a weekly coming together, worshipping together, eating together, and praying together to understand that without one another there can be no meal and no Eucharistic sacrifice. That without the community, the words of Jesus rings hollow. He didn't gather one person alone, He gathered the many. He didn't send one person to go out and spread the word alone, He sent the many.

The parable illustrates that we can be blown off our own life's course if we allow our direction to be determined by the winds of the day. The sailor knew that his experience with the tools given to him to keep him safe were enough for the trip to be taken. He didn't allowed the elements of this world to pull him astray. The Gospel is pointing out the same thing about Jesus. If we can allow Jesus to steer our boat of life, then maybe we too can explore the avenues that are waiting for us.

<u>SALVATION</u>

Nature of Sin

Gospel – Mark 7:1 – 23

References – Matthew 32:12; Ephesians 2:10; 1st Peter 5:5

There once was a town that was divided. It wasn't divided by streets not so much as the side of which street one grew up and lived on. It wasn't divided by language not so much as everyone in that town spoke the same dialect but spoke with different hidden meanings behind everything they said. It wasn't even divided by age not so much as there were people of all ages on each side of the town.

The town was divided by ideology. There were those that held a firm belief in the literal interpretation of the bible and those that believed that everything in that same bible was to be interpreted through the current day's attitudes. Each person in the town had picked which side of the religious debate they were going to live by and there was no crossing over. And when the two sides did meet, there was generally a lot of name calling and yelling that commenced.

One day, an evangelist came to town. He first visited the literalists and then the relativists. After visiting both side, he called the two sides together for a meeting. In this meeting, the evangelist brought up the inerrancy of the bible, how many parts were historically inaccurate because there were no historians around to write them. He brought up how many parts were, indeed, literal as there really was a historical Jesus.

The evangelist went down the whole list of those things which the two sides were at war with each other over. And then, when the meeting was ending, the evangelist spoke of the two commandments by Jesus to both sides.

Now, if the many sides we have today could come to an agreement that each side is both literal in their steadfastness and unwillingness to listen and be a neighbor and both are figurative in their outlook on what the other side really thought. Maybe the world would be more at peace.

****

The Pharisee's created all these rules and regulations based on the notion that, by observing them, it would remind every Jew that he was set apart. That they were special. And that every Jew would be allowed to enter the kingdom of heaven based on his or her faithful observance of those rules, or redefined traditions.

But what it turned out to be was a set of rules that held everyone down rather than lift them up and when Jesus came on the scene, and His message was about lifting the individual up, well that didn't sit very well with the established order.

But Jesus came back to let the Jews know that what they were following was not what He needed them to do. This resulted in this nagging feeling that maybe they, the Jews, weren't measuring up. Not doing enough. Not sacrificing enough. Not praying enough times of the day.

But, unlike the Pharisees and Jews of Jesus' day, we have solid proof in the bread of life. The body of Jesus and it's this Jesus that says to us that even though we're not perfect, we're accepted by God because we're accepted by Jesus.

It's only because we're broken that Jesus even bothered to come down in the first place. And that's why what defiles God is what comes out of our hearts rather than what goes in the mouth.

Theology is a ubiquitous term. Many folks think it means one thing while it really intones another. Theology, plain and simple, is the study of God. Now we have two major types of theology in our Christian world today, the theology of glory and the theology of the law.

The theology of glory is more commonly referred to as prosperity Gospel, or as I like to call it, Gospel lite. Except that it never gives light that last – only a glimmer that shines for the moment and then ultimately fades into the darkness from whence it came.

The theology of the law is what the Pharisees were practicing. It's a theology with so many rules and regulations that it drove out the real meaning of what Christ came back to us to deliver – Love your God with all your heart, your mind and your soul and love your neighbor as yourself.

Both sides to these theologies are flawed inherently in that if one ascribes to either in totality then one neglects the other. The theology of glory says we'll be blessed with abundant worldly goods if only we do this or that enough. The theology of the law says we'll get to heaven if we follow this rule or that rule enough. Both start out really good and hopeful but neither ever seems to be enough.

But there is a third – the theology of the cross. This came out of Luther's Heidelberg Disputation way back in 1518 so it has been around for a while. It says that no matter what we do, we can never reach heaven or God or Jesus on our own. It says that since we can't begin to live with the idea that what we do falls short because we're not perfect, we end up hating the action to begin with.

Jesus is saying that the solution to the disease of sin that the Pharisees were trying to wash away is the revolution that they can't get rid of that sin to begin with no matter how many times they wash, or pray, or do their religious traditional stuff. It's simply not within their power. Not within their will. Never was – never will be.

That's our good news though. That even though we try and try and try again to get it right, our will just doesn't get the job done but our faith in Jesus allows us to be assured that we can reach our destination. We no longer have to wonder what we gotta do to walk down that line, get down off that elevator to the streets of heaven, and enter through those gates.

The parable illustrates that if one goes too far to the left or the right then one become blind to the middle. Grace is that gift that recognizes that there are laws and there are moments when nuance must be present. Grace recognizes that despite what we want, we can never actually exist in either camp, left or right. This parable shows the dangers when humans determine what is morally right or wrong.

SALVATION

Where's the Beef?

Gospel – John 6:22 – 35

References – Exodus 16:18; Isaiah 55; Matthew 6:19; Matthew 19:14

There once was a really great restaurant that everyone in town just loved to go. Their menu included the ordinary things one would find on a menu but every Friday night they would list something special and the rule was that to get the very best, you had to go on those Friday nights.

But, one week, there was no listing. Nothing on the menu that was not already there the other six days and the regular customers just didn't know what to do. Their taste buds were all geared up for that special surprise they had grown used to.

When the owner was questioned as to why there wasn't anything like the specials on the menu, the owner said that the chef that had done these specials had taken a job across town. He said the chef had complained but he had ignored those complaints. The owner said that he only realized his mistake a few days later but couldn't get the chef back.

So the restaurant's patrons left and went to the other place where the chef was and soon the original restaurant closed due to not enough business. The owner of that restaurant realized that his employees were ones to be valued because without that treatment, his customers would leave and he would have nothing.

Unfortunately, like the people in Jesus' day and many of us, we all come to that realization later rather than sooner and the end result is that we all go hungry.

****

Our Gospel harkens back to a time when the people had skewed views of what the miracles of Jesus were all about. Whether it be about water or bread or wine or fish they just couldn't wrap their heads around the miracles of Jesus and that Jesus was the Messiah.

But they were only concerned that their bellies were full and they were quick to discount the gift by God. They only saw Jesus as the consummate waiter bringing them the latest catch of the day. Serving them as though they were the masters and he was a common servant.

Not understanding that the "Bread of Life" that Jesus was talking about was not the manna like their ancestors had, not the loaves that the little boy had brought, but the Bread of Life that Jesus was talking about. And that was Him. That through Him, we'll never be hungry. Never be thirsty. Never be searching for that meaning we all want out of life.

But we do the same today, as they did then, with both of our sacraments. When we eat of the bread, when we come forward to take the bread and dip it in the wine, many have long sense forgotten what that symbolism is. The beauty is, that because this is also a gift from God, there are no requirements or conditions that have to be met to come to the table. Just enjoy.

Just be a part of something no one probably understood then either but since they were all invited by Jesus, just as you and I are every Sunday or on most days even, they went, they participated. And that's why Jesus is the Bread of Life. That's why Jesus is the true bread from heaven given by God to all who come forward.

So, in our Gospel, the people searched Him out when they found He was missing. But He really was with them all along. Just not in their physical presence on that grassy knoll. And He is with us here, today, sitting next to us.

So, in this Gospel, I don't believe that the folks there got it. They really didn't get that the miracle by Jesus, of the gift, was just that, a gift. They were equating what Jesus did for them and what they must do, in kind, as a sort of works based faith. The people 2,000 plus years ago, on that grassy knoll, saw Jesus but forgot their history.

The parable illustrates that where we put our value will cause our own lives to take turns for the worse or the better. As in Jesus' day, the people there also wouldn't come to grips with what was right before them and, as a result, suffered. They had to go the extra mile in order to get back into His presence. We can be as guilty because those closest to us have value that we can hang onto but many times forget that or overlook it.

<u>SERVING</u>

So – What Have You Done Lately?

Gospel – Matthew 25:14 – 30
References – Matthew 22:37 – 39

There once was a young girl who was born with a very high IQ. Her score was over 200 which was 60 points above the most notable person considered a genius, Albert Einstein. This girl was kept from the public eye because her parents didn't want her to be subject to all the public relations that would eventually surround her. They were afraid of what it might cause to her childhood.

She went to a normal public school and surrounded herself with all the things children do. She played games with her classmates but never let on just how smart she really was. She carried her parents fear with her.

However, when she grew up, she also failed to use her wisdom to better others. She failed to help those who would benefit from her knowledge of a vast array of subjects. So she ultimately failed in her first marriage. She ultimately failed in doing anything that would expand her life so others could overcome theirs. She was afraid of the limelight. Afraid of something she did not know was true.

Ultimately, this remarkable woman would finally be forced into the limelight when her IQ scores were published. It was only then, many year later, that her knowledge aided her new husband to develop a mechanical artificial heart that would go on to help many others. That and her desire to write on subjects that would impact other people's lives.

She was quoted as saying partly, "I think we all bear a great responsibility to give back to society. We cannot give as much as we can gain." You see, it was only through living outside her own self that she was able to discover and experience the glorious gift of knowledge that God granted to her and begin to live through herself to others.

****

What have we done that expands our own relationship with the one who created us? The one who gave up His only Son just so we could come together and have the security and confidence that we can live on in eternity forever? What have we done that expands the kingdom of God just like the talents the master gave his slaves? Enable others to receive even a portion of those talents we've been given? What have we done with the time that we have left, here on this earth, to lift one another up in ways that will live on even after we're gone?

Sometimes it's real hard to clear our heads to get a good look at what each gift is the gift each of us really has. What blessings we've been given. What talents we can share. It's gonna be real hard to come to grips with our own mortality because our own pasts are filled with times that we'd rather forget. Our own present is filled with uncertainty because of all the forces that want to drag us down into the depths of deceit. Our own futures are anyone's guess as to what will be force fed to us.

But, sometimes, what we're faced with is outside our immediate control but, much of the time, all that uncertainty, all that grief, all those memories are things that we have imposed on ourselves.

But what the people 2,000 plus years ago had was a great sense of community in the micro sense. Many would come together to celebrate. To gather around those in their community and spread the good news so that all would benefit.

How else could you explain the desire and the directed actions of those who wanted even the lowest of the low, us, to have

the words printed so we could use them, learn from them, get
and become inspired within them today? In each of those time
periods, the people of that time had to deal with much of what
we deal with today.

The parable of the ten talents, in this Gospel, goes deep and
should force us to ask the questions of what do we do with our
own gifts. Specifically, Jesus is using this to point out that
each of the talents is a part of our own life. But think of it as a
day in our own lives. A day in which we can choose to make it
gleam with the light of God and His truths or shrink with
Satan's deceit leaving us in fear.

And the two slaves that took those talents given to them and
multiplied them is Jesus illustrating for the people that God
has given you your own tomorrows to multiply too. Or, we can
be like the one slave that hid his away and Jesus is clear on
the consequences of that too.

Jesus points out that while our gifts that God has given to us
may differ, our opportunities for doing something with these
gifts to the world at large and our communities are the same.
But, no path we go down will be without challenge. A risk.

We'll run the risk that someone out there, on social media, will
take offense at the truth. And there might be consequences.

We'll run the risk that what we're charged to do, minister to others, might be hampered by some edict from up on high.

But Jesus is saying, right here, take the risk. Take the gamble. Take a shot. It could be surmised that the last servant, who only returned what was given to him, operated out of fear. Operated out of a lack of trust or belief in God. It's interesting to note that all of the stories in the Bible have more to do with our trust in God rather than whether God is all knowing or not. The real question is "Do we have the trust needed to allow God to operate in our own lives?"

Our answers to ourselves will tell us which servant we truly are. Our answers can point to us our patterns of living out our lives. Jesus is asking each of us what have we done with our own talents that support and embolden the love your neighbor part.

This Gospel points out that there will be a day of reckoning and it's here that those that have done nothing with their "talents" or their treasures will receive nothing in return. Our trust in God with what we've been given enables us to be one of the first two in this Gospel and not the last. Folks, we've been given many talents. We can use them or store them away. Either way, we'll be asked for them when the final days are here.

The parable illustrates how we can allow the world to tell us what we are not worth. We focus in on that and it affects all our tomorrows. It's only when we break free and begin to use the gifts that we've been given by God that we can begin to see the impact our lives have with others. The girl in the parable shows that when she becomes ruled by her gifts in order to lift others up then she becomes all that she was born to be.

<u>SERVING</u>

What is My End Motivation?

Gospel – Matthew 20:1 – 16
References – Matthew 19:16

Once there were two workers in an auto factory. The first, which I'll call Bob, had been there for many years. The second, which I'll call Steve, just got hired about a month ago. Economic times, being what they were, the factory decided that it had to let some people on the floor go.

After many meetings among the senior management, they decided that the best person to let go would be Bob. They would give him a generous severance package that included 6 months paid wages among other things. Now the union that Bob belonged to proceeded to object, saying that his longevity with the company gave him tenure. That Steve, the newest person hired, should be the first to go but the company kept to their decisions.

Soon enough, this matter went to arbitration. Threats of a strike were made and threats for lawsuits were also made. But the factory kept to their decision and won out in the end. The reason, the factory was privately owned and it was the owner's decision because it was the owner that had sole ownership of that factory.

The owner's decision was decided because Bob, the one with the most seniority, would be able, and did, find another place to work sooner because of his experience and his knowledge of the assembly line at the owner's factory whereas Steve, being relatively new, would have remained unemployed the longest. The end result was that both were employed.

****

What do we want out of this life? What do we think we're gonna get after we die? Is the world fair? Are we fair with those around us? Do we travel down the road of least resistance? Do we go down the road that gives us the most challenges?

Now, as we live our lives, we like, or believe, that what we do has a bigger purpose. I mean, we probably don't spend all of our waking time mulling over if what we've done is part of a bigger picture. We pretty much like to think that what we've accomplish has a contribution to everything going on around us.

You see, this passage isn't about money, isn't about anything physically on this earth, but about grace. God's grace. It's about the fact that there ain't nothing you or I can do, how hard we work, what we think, or anything else that determines the level or amount of grace that God has for us. It's up to Him and Him alone.

Now, some will sit here and think, but I've been to church my whole life. I'm a mature Christian. I haven't broken any rules. I'm here and ready. And then some will think, man, I just turned my life over to Jesus. Maybe I'm not worthy to get in. Maybe I need to do more in order that His favor might come on down for me.

But, the point that Jesus was making to all of this is that it is God and God alone that decides what will be our recompense. That it's not a matter of equal grace for equal discipleship. Equal grace for equal work. Now folks, it's not about what you do that's visible, how many long years or hours you put into this whole Jesus thing that matters, it's not what you do that ultimately matters to God and Christ but what you have not done.

This passage is about the grace that the owner of the field, God, has determined that each is worth so it really deserves to be on the side of Gospel in our law and Gospel theology. This passage really boils down to this. No matter what you do, how hard you pray, how much you contribute, if you are using those things to elevate yourself then you've become like the first workers.

The parable illustrates that what we do in the service of God should be done in a way that does not elevate us but, rather, elevates the people we are serving. If we're doing it to look good or to score points then we're not serving but self-dealing. God is calling all of us to be a person that works for the kingdom. We all end up in heaven if we are believers. No matter if one has been that believer for years or one is brand new. The reward is the same.

<u>SIGNS</u>

Belief Seeking Human Understanding

Gospel – Mark 9:1 – 13
References – Exodus 33:7

There once was a young girl that would take almost everything she earned and go down to skid row where she would give it all to the homeless people there. This caused her parents much anxiety as they thought that place to be unsafe.

They would speak with the girl but, sure enough, on the day she would get her earnings, she would be back over there. Her parents wouldn't go themselves because they felt the people there, for the most part, could help themselves and they just chose not to.

But the young girl made no such judgments. Her parents would even try to put up barriers, of all sorts, in the young girl's path but the moment she was unencumbered, she went back. They would take away all her earnings but the young girl would find other odd jobs around the neighborhood and take what she made and go. She did this over and over and over again. She would go regardless of what was put in her life to keep her away.

Finally, out of desperation, her parents followed her to her destination. Sure enough, they saw her give what money she had to the various homeless people but then they saw the homeless people go into the local corner store and come out with not alcohol or drugs or any other nefarious items but with bread and juice and other staple items and proceed to give it to many of the other homeless people.

When the parents finally asked one of the homeless about that, he told them that the store owner would match whatever the girl gave them out of the owner's sense of generosity. The store owner had heard of the young girl's commitment and that inspired him to be just as committed and that allowed the people to multiply the gifts of the girl so many more could have something to eat.

****

Do we define our belief by what we can see or do we define it by what's in our hearts? It's really a deeper question than it seems because what we want is to be able to get our heads around what believing means.

Sometimes, though, what we feel is stuck so far back that it takes an event to bring it the surface. Sometimes we're afraid to show what and how we truly feel. Peter was a lot of action.

He almost always said what was on his mind. But sometimes we can't be like Peter because of consequences to those around us.

So, regardless of how you may interpret what the scriptures have to say, regardless if they fit what is considered to be popular, regardless if they conflict with what we want them to be, they are the stories that tell us who is ultimately in charge.

Now, the transfiguration of Jesus really has two sides. One of the sides is the person being transfigured from without and the other is transfigured from within. Each of us has to decide which side we're on. Honestly decide which we will be. On the outside or on the inside.

Being transfigured from without is being defined by those around you. Being defined by whatever and whomever is telling you what you are. Trying to live up to the expectations of those around you. Trying to match all that those around you have determined you should be.

Being transfigured from within is where you begin to let your heart affect your mind so much so that the true words of God are showing you what He desires for you to be. It's where, despite everyone around you saying one thing, you know what's speaking to you from within and that's the road you go down.

Our youth have this constant dilemma facing them. They're surrounded by a cadre of stimulations that are all telling them that to fit in, to be in the in crowd, to be cool, you gotta smoke this or drink that or do things that you really know better.

They can be manipulated by very sophisticated buzz words and those leave their mark. They carry those messages forward into adulthood and the end result is that we have a whole generation of young adults that look at phantasy as reality because their reality is relevant. Except it has zero relevance.

Folks that's what the kids today are being told and sold. That Jesus is some fairy tale and to just stop and get away because to follow Him is exclusive to what someone else might feel and that would make you a person who was bigoted or xenophobic.

Now, I say this is what the kids are faced with but, in reality, it's exactly what you and me are faced with on a day to day basis too. We're really called to choose which side of the coin we will become when we're transfigured. When we're transformed. When we're looking at our own situation and trying to figure out where we fit into this whole scheme of life.

But you can make a conscious decision. You can chose to hold out for the promise that is the truth or live for whatever the world is offering you. You can be transfigured and transformed just like Jesus because, like Jesus, the truth of God is really declared and embedded in you.

Folks, it really doesn't matter what time in your life that you'll be faced with this world that's attempting to change you, transform you into something that they can then use to fulfill their kingdom on earth. It also holds true that everyone, in whatever time of their life, can choose to be reborn and transformed thereby being transfigured from within like Jesus. As God designed you in your very DNA to be.

We can be lifted up through our own transformations which transfigures us but only through the life giving words of God. And it's only through that life giving word of God that we can face the world to keep ourselves from ever becoming as the world wants us to be. We can be filled with the grace and mercy of God so much so that we'll begin to put on the glowing white clothes of righteousness that we can then claim as our own.

The parable illustrates that the young girl is one that was transformed from within because she saw the possibility of the people in front of her. Of humanity. That allows her to be transformed from within because she's counting on the fact that people are innately good and hate to see others suffer. It's not until her parents come down to where she is that they begin to be transformed too.

I believe that a bit of the young girl is in all of us. What I see many do tells me that it is so. But I also believe that there is a great amount of her parents in us too. It's refreshing to see the times that the young girl wins and not the parents.

<u>SIGNS</u>

Doubt

Gospel – Mark 4:35 – 41
References – Jeremiah 29

There once was a boy who had a problem with stuttering. He would start to stutter when he was very nervous. All through his life people would either discount what he had to say or just walk away because it took too long for him to express what he wanted to say. All because of the stuttering problem.

Then, he grew up and was tasked with having to speak to many people. He was overcome with doubt and fear. Fear that he would look foolish in front of the public and doubt that he could get through what he had to say but the people were counting on him to give them courage. How could he do this when he had little courage of his ability himself?

So he practiced what he would say. He went over it over and over again. He spent days just repeating the words in his speech. It was very important for him to get it right. But he also found himself disappointed in himself because he just couldn't seem to speak without that stutter.

Then a teacher came into his life and taught him to put himself outside of himself. To not look for a solution to his problem but to rely on the points he wanted to make and just say what was in his heart rather than what was on the paper. When he spoke from his heart, that took control rather than his mind which doubted his being.

True enough, the man spoke from his heart to a nation that was listening and that brought everyone who was listening great courage because they heard what was really important. And this was during the time of a World War when everyone needed to have the courage to dispel the doubts that they could survive.

****

You know – that lingering question that we all get, from time to time, when something happens that just doesn't quite fit. Doesn't quite add up. It happens when we least expect it and it can be a good thing or a very long lasting disability. We suffer doubt alone and/or in groups.

We express our doubts outwardly or withhold it within which then turns into a kind of self-defeating ideology and can overcome anything and everything positive in any relationship. We just don't know exactly how to handle the doubt exactly.

Doubt is defined as a feeling of uncertainty or lack of conviction. A fear or suspect. A lack of confidence in your own decisions or distrust in something or someone or someone else's decision.

The church is not immune to all levels of doubt. After all, if it were not for the history of doubts there would've been no Council of Nicaea or the establishment of creeds or even the writings of the Gospels themselves. There would've been no reformation.

In the early days, there would've been little reason for Jesus to travel around and do the miracles He did. It was precisely the instilling of the doubts by the Jewish leaders that allowed the early Jesus followers to hold on to the truth and promises of what Jesus was giving to them.

We read that Thomas, you know doubting Thomas, seems to be the most prominent one in all of the Gospels that had doubt. The fact of the matter is that he has gotten a raw deal. The reality is that all of the disciples were so full of doubt that it almost sunk the boat they were on in this Gospel and caused them to not see Jesus walking right beside them on the road to Emmaus.

And when God doesn't seem to show up, we become disillusioned. We settle for the age old mantra that God is absent, that He doesn't care. We forget that God is not a waiter at a restaurant ready to take our order from the menu of life in front of us. This passage speaks to the very core of what we all experience with Jesus sitting right there next to us. A mistaken view that He's not listening, not caring.

Many equate doubt with a lack of faith. While the two, doubt and faith, are related in a sense – they are very different in nature. I prefer to believe that my own doubts allow me to know more about God and Jesus and how I can walk with people.

The real message within this passage is that Jesus is always there, will always be there, and is constantly working to heal our brokenness. Our doubts. The point is that all we really need to do is to let go and let live. Be assured that Christ is there in our corner.

Our doubt is the yield signs of our lives. It can be a direction that leads us to a safer space within the confines of God's family or it can be a road that leads us down the path of those that cannot seem to see that Jesus is inviting them in to trust Him and rely on Him.

The parable illustrates that when you go outside of yourself to something bigger than yourself, great things can happen. The purpose of doubt is to instill fear so that we cannot do that which we were designed to be. The parable says that there is something bigger than each of us and to rely on that and great things can and most often do happen so that everyone can be lifted up.

<u>SIGNS</u>

Expectations

Gospel – Luke 24:36 – 53

There once was a goat that spent his days totally unaware of anything that went on around him. He was content to play and eat and eat and play each and every day. But one day, another goat came into the pasture and the first goat thought he could make friends.

He would go up to the other goat and rub up against it to show his friendship. But the newer goat would have nothing of it. The newer goat would turn and butt his head and hurt the first goat. This made the first goat very sad so he looked for other ways to create a friendship.

What the first goat didn't know was that the second goat had been brought from a farm where the owner beat him. Starved him. Secluded him. And because of that, the second goat had no way of knowing what the first goat had in mind because he was taught to be cautious of every other thing around him. He was taught to trust no one and nothing.

Same with us many times. And some never get that chance to form a lasting relationship that's good. Jesus came to show us that it's possible to repair our own histories so that our futures can be blessed.

****

Expectations. You know, this passage speaks about expectations not always being our realities. That sometimes what we think we know ain't necessarily so. That many times, what we have learned has to be relearned in order for us to grow in our own faith journeys.

And I'm also reminded that sometimes our own histories of relationships and fears and memories can keep us from seeing what is evidently right in front of our noses. You know, the proverbial forest for the trees?

Jesus promised the disciples that He would be with them always. He promised them that He would return. He says it when He speaks about the fulfillment of the Law of Moses, the prophets, and in the Psalms.

But I think that sometimes we let our own worldview intrude on the world that Jesus is talkin' about. We have a hard time filtering out all the worldviews in lieu of the views that Jesus is talkin' about.

A worldview that says buy this, and you'll be happy. A worldview that says be this, and people will like you. A worldview that says do this, and you can live a life of ease. A worldview that says be sure and accommodate everyone's opinion so no one gets offended. A worldview that puts the things of this world over and above the things of God.

Of course, we're human. We're no different than those eleven disciples sitting there. They had to see to truly believe. I'm quite sure that Thomas wasn't the only one who doubted the veracity of Jesus' truth. After all, wasn't it Peter that went fishing after the crucifixion?

But we can renew our trust. We can re-live out the promises of Jesus week after week at the communion table. We can renew our faith on a daily basis by the remembrance of our baptism. The trust in the words given to us by Jesus that we repeat here, in the sanctuary, week after week.

I read this passage and I think, Jesus is talking to me. Jesus is walking with me. Jesus is talking to you. Jesus is walking with you now. As sure as I'm standing here, the Gospel of Luke was written for us, to give us strength, to give us courage.

You see Jesus has come. He is risen. And He has risen for me, for you, for all of those with whom we're charged by the power of the Holy Spirit in ministering to, in shepherding to, in spreading the good news of that resurrection to.

This passage talks of the promise to us that Jesus has come, Jesus was crucified, Jesus is risen. The beauty of the cross is not that Jesus hung there, but that He came down, He came back to us, and He is with us now, at this very moment. The beauty of the cross is that it is empty.

This passage says that we can put our trust in the truth and the light that is Jesus Christ. This passage says that by putting our trust in the life and the words of Christ, we will be blessed with the power of the Holy Spirit. Christ promises that we can have joy in sharing this Good news with anyone and everyone we meet regardless of the consequences because of our trust in Him. He did come back to His disciples and He has come back for us too. Christ words of promise were true then and His promises are true now.

The parable is about us being the second goat and Jesus the first. It's about how Jesus keeps trying to get to us. Trying to befriend us. About how we allow our pasts to shape our futures and cut off any attempts to make a connection. This parable is about how, if we can just let it all go, we can enjoy the company and blessings of Jesus in our lives.

<u>SIGNS</u>

Imagine That

Gospel – Mark 6:30 – 44, 53 – 56
References – Mark 6:45 – 52

There once was a teen who grew up and spent his whole life on a farm. Every day, while he was young, his father had told him to never cross the fence between his farm and the neighbor to his east. His father told him that there were people there who would shoot him if he ever crossed that line. So the teen obeyed his father and never questioned him about it.

As the teen got older he went to class in the rather small school. But one day a new girl arrived. No one had ever seen her and she looked like she needed a friend. So the teen decided that he would get to know her. She wouldn't say where she lived or where she came from so that remained a mystery and the teen never pressured her for those answers.

As the both of them got to know each other they came to really like each other. As one school year ended and another started, the teen would always look for this girl in the classrooms. Finally, on the last day of their twelfth year, the teen asked again where the girl lived and where she came from.

She finally relented and told him. It was from the area that the teen's father had told him to never go. But what the teen found out was the area he was forbidden to venture into held great promises that his heart needed to be filled with. The girl that he had grown to love.

The unknown satisfied the empty place in his person and it wasn't until he got to know what he was not supposed to know that he found that what he really needed to know was there all along. We will miss the opportunity too if we cannot learn to listen and see.

****

Why is this Gospel important? It's because Jesus is there taking care of the needs of the people. He's there to satisfy them in their time of need. It shows that Jesus can feed many on the fruits of the few if the few will just allow Him to do His work.

It also shows that no earthly roadblock can keep Jesus from coming to us. And it shows that no matter how astounding His works might be, no matter how many times He cures the sick, feeds the thousands, walks on water, we humans, in our brokenness, just can't seem to understand the fuller picture.

The totality of what He does and says and shows to us is sometimes missing from our field of view. But we can try and get a glimpse. We can keep touching His garment in the smallest of hope that His peace and mercy and glory will somehow move to us.

The shore that Christ walked off that boat then to be in the lives of those people then is the same Christ that is here with us now setting foot on our life's shores. Speaking to us through these Gospels. That shore that Christ walked onto then is the same door that He is knocking on right here, right now. The door to your heart. The door to your soul.

We face many challenges in our day to day lives. Many days are hard to get out of bed even. But never you doubt that Christ is there walking with you through all those challenges and all those times when you may feel alone. He's with us whether we're experiencing joy or pain. He's with us.

I believe that the lesson for today's Gospel is that in order for us to spread the message that Christ is alive in each of us, that in order for others to understand the message that Christ is with us, that in order for this Gospel to take root and spread like a wild fire, it must be told and shared and given away often.

Folks, we're no different than the people of Jesus' time. We want to hear the good news that He came to give just as they did. We want to know that we are accepted into the kingdom of God just as they did. We want to know that His grace and His mercy are ours for the taking and that it's promised to us just as they did.

The parable illustrates that we can become so embedded in what we've heard that our ears can turn off what we will hear. The teen finally found his love by finding the object of that love in the forbidden places of his heart and mind. The father never told him the why only the what. It's when we can fill in the places that broken humans leave empty that our own hearts can begin to believe on the faith we've been given.

<u>SIGNS</u>

Is Our Oil for Our House or Our Heart?

Gospel – Matthew 25:1 – 13
References – John 3:20

Two men were in a 2 mile foot race. As the day of the race drew near, each of these men trained in a very different way. One would run miles to build up his stamina. The other would work out on a tread mill. One would go to different parts of the country to experience the landscape while the other viewed parts of the world on a screen attached to the tread mill.

Each of these men trained every day for this event. Each of these men were in fit shape on the day of the race. During the first mile of this race both of the men were neck and neck. One would pull out ahead and then the other. During the second mile of the race, the first man, the one that ran the training miles on roads, began to pull out ahead. The second man, the one who used the treadmill, started to lag. As the finish line got closer, the first ended up way ahead of the second and eventually won the race.

You see, the course that they had to run on that race day was filled with pot holes and impediments. The first man was prepared for this as he encountered them in his training while the second man never came across them because his training, on the treadmill, never allowed him to encounter the hardships and challenges that comes with real life events. The second man never experienced the reality of what he would face while the first man was truly prepared.

****

You know, we all find ourselves subconsciously thinking we always have tomorrow. Whether that's putting off a vacation or a visit or even something that needs to get done around the house. There's always tomorrow, right? Tomorrow's a tricky thing. But what if today was all we got?

This Gospel is all about those end times. Some may think we're living through those times right now, with what we see in the media. Some may think that tomorrow will forever change in a way that's so foreign to what today is that it's unbearable. Some may also think tomorrow will bring a time of renewal and relief. That new possibilities are just over the horizons. I don't know which you are. That's for you to think about.

But I do know that what this Gospel is telling us – we should be ready. Not for some outcome on the political landscape or anything, but to be ready for when it really counts. Put aside the earthly trials of today for heavenly preparation. Be ready for when Jesus will come back here and we'll all have to answer to Him. Because He's coming you know.

Whether we consciously think about it or not, He's coming never the less. Whether we're ready for Him or not, He's coming back. Whether you or I are anxious or nervous about it or not, He's coming back never the less. And our Gospel asks each of us whether we're those bridesmaids that didn't think to bring enough oil for their lamps or are we the ones that are prepared.

The bridesmaids, if you haven't figured it out yet, is us. The church. The ecclesia. We're the bridesmaids. We're the ones who are supposed to be ready for the eschatology, the end times. We're the ones that Jesus created to gather together in order that His good news could be spread.

But we also have the oil. The liquid that courses through our veins. The bridesmaids, who were shut out of the wedding feast, are the ones that only brought enough to serve themselves, only had enough coursing through their veins for themselves. The oil is the symbol, here, for what we've done for others.

The bridegroom is Jesus. He closes the door not because those five don't believe but because their oil has been kept, been withheld, for themselves and the light of their lamp, their light, has been extinguished.

You know it's easy. Somethings get put off and then it gets easier and easier to move them further and further into the future. It becomes comfortable. And soon enough, they never get done. But Jesus says to do it now and I will say that once you get in there and start to do what you're supposed to do, fulfilling that goal, then you look back and it really wasn't that big of a time taker.

The oil belonging to the five that got locked out is like the oil in all of us. We can let it burn out so that we end up in the dark or we can make sure that we have enough to do what we're supposed to do. Give light for our ability to see that the Savior is coming back for us.

Letting us into the banquet where our own oil will no longer be needed because that very banquet is forever lit with the presence of the only one that can reach into us and hold us and give us the peace we all so desperately need and want. A banquet that we're drawn to by the very light that gives the real power to each of our lamps here on this earth.

We can put off till tomorrow what should be done today forever being surprised by the ways that our God has of showing us that tomorrow is not what He wants. Or we can sleep in the comfort of knowing that our lamps are full if we have prepared and become open to what we're called to do.

The parable illustrates that we say maybe tomorrow. Maybe someday. Maybe I'll get around to it. But here it's very clear, that day may never come. It's like the second guy in our parable. The one that prepared himself for the race of his life using methods that didn't present to him the realities of the race. And, unlike the first guy who had to go through the troubles along his path, the second guy decided to stay home. Decided to hold onto his oil, his words, his actions to be in the comfort of the house all by himself.

<u>SIGNS</u>

The Lost Seeking the Found

Gospel – Matthew 2:1 – 12

There once was a traveler who made it his life's mission to record the histories of all of civilizations. The things people have told through the ages but had never put down in writing. Things thought to be lost from one generation to another.

This traveler would visit various parts of the world and record the stories of the people there. Many times he would sit with people far away from the rest of civilization and would record their stories and tell other stories that he had previously been told.

The traveler was so well know, after many years, that when news of his pending arrival would reach an area, huge throngs of people would come together. Have a banquet together. And discuss and debate what stories they would tell the traveler so he could record them down for all of history.

At the end of many of his years, on the road talking with people, the traveler had quite the large collection of tales. And in this collection, he found that the people he met, the people he had caused to gather, became more familiar with their own histories because they retold the stories handed down from generation to generation that would have been otherwise lost from generation to generation in preparation for retelling them to him and, in this way, many histories of those communities were relived and relished.

****

Sometimes, we should look back on our relationship with Christ and be assured that what we have chosen is still the right course of action. Sometimes, what we have, though, can come with good times and bad times and it is human nature to ask God if you still matter to Him. Sometimes, because we have been broken, we tend to just close our eyes to the possibilities and then we are smacked with reality when we try to focus. Epiphany is the season to do just that.

Many of us prefer the darkness and denial to the light of reality. You see, our present is just a reflection on our past. And the past of those that came before us. We can also take a good look at the people who've come before and gain an epiphany to help us tomorrow.

The magi who searched for the Messiah, the Christ child, were men who escaped their world, in the East, to find fulfillment to the story of what is the truth. We're not sure of the exact number of magi since the number three was chosen because of the number of gifts brought to Jesus. The gist is that these guys travel many months and at great cost to themselves to get to where the alignment of very bright planets would tell them that the beginning of the end days had begun.

Now, Herod the Great, an Iduman, conquered his own people. He put down any dissent that existed and he did it with such brutality that he was made famous for it in his own right among rulers in the provinces of Rome. He was in league with the Scribes who were a professional class of experts in the religious and civil laws of the Bible and Jewish traditions. Herod was also aligned with the Pharisees, sometimes referred to as Chief Priests. They too were of the upper ruling class associated with the Temple.

In the late third century, men would leave all that they had and go out into the deserts of Arabia. Egypt and Syria to be more precise. They would do this in order that they could gain a better understanding of the words that were handed to them by their religious leaders. They belonged to a group called the monastics.

This movement grew and grew and the end result was that whole communities would spring up around that single lone man. The movement grew at such a pace that many of the original men would then have to escape again only to see it happen over and over. But what the loners, the monastics, were seeking was within them all the time.

They, like Herod, wanted confirmation that their way of thinking was correct. That their sufferings was what Jesus wanted. That by escaping, they came closer to God.

In ancient mythology, fable, allegory and truth there exists the tale of the Holy Grail. Romantics, authors and film writers, alike, paint a gathering of men who would ride off into the sunset in search of this ancient relic. The Knights Templars was one such monastic order. The quest for the Holy Grail, by the Templars, was really a quest for recognition of something to be found.

What each of these has in common is the common desire by every human being to find something that's lost. Find meaning in some obligatory history that holds imaginations firm. Find what is lost to many within their very souls.

The sounds around us can convince us that what we cannot possibly be grasped by the God of all time cannot be accepted because we're broken without redemption. But Jesus coming into our lives is the proof that even though we seek that which cannot possibly be explained, no amount of pressure by this broken world can obliterate the promise that everything we seek is right before our touch.

The parable illustrates that the real stories that we seek are those of our loved ones that are all around us. If only we can ask. The man collecting the stories found that the more people told their own histories the more it became alive for not only them but all those around them.

This Gospel is like that. It tells of a story sought out but later realized when the truth became known. We are like those Magi in that we think we must seek something out that is greater than ourselves when the reality is that all we need to become known is what we have by our sides each and every day.

<u>SIGNS</u>

Trusting God's Unending Rule

Gospel – Luke 1:26 – 38

References – 2nd Corinthians 12:9

This is a true story of a man called Marcel Sternberger who gets into a train in Brooklyn on the subway and it's in the middle of the day. He'd gone to visit a sick friend who was dying. He visited the sick friend and takes this train that he doesn't ever take because he doesn't live there and also it's the middle of the day and he's normally at work. He gets into the train and it's crowded. But as soon as he gets in, one man gets off and there's one seat left and he makes a bee line for it and sits down.

But the man next to him is reading a newspaper with his arms out stretched so Sternberger, sort of craning his neck away, looks at the newspaper and it's in Polish. And Sternberger understood Polish. So he's starting to read it and he notices the man is reading it from the classified section.

So he looks at the man and he says, "Are you looking for a job sir?" And the man said, "No, I'm not looking for a job, I'm looking for my wife." Sternberger says, "What do you mean?

Are you looking to find somebody to marry?" The man said,
"No, no, no, I'm from Hungary. Debrekenen Hungary. During
the war, I was taken away by the Russians to bury the
German dead and by the time I came back, my city had been
liberated but I was not sure whether my wife ended up in a
concentration camp in Auschwitz or whether she was
liberated."

He continues, "I've had no contact with her so I've come to
America looking for my wife. To see if she was liberated and
brought here. We have no contact address for each other."
Marcel Sternberger starts to think, "You know what? A few
days ago I was at a party." He was talking to himself now.
"And there was a woman from Debrekenen Hungary who said
she'd been liberated by the Allies and brought to the United
States and her husband had been taken by the Soviets to bury
the German dead." And he'd written her name down because
he said maybe we'll get together some time.

Then he turns to the man next to him and says to him, "Sir,
what's your wife's name?" "He says, Maria, Maria Paskin."
Sternberger takes out that piece of paper and it says, Maria
Paskin and has the phone number. And then he says to the
man next to him and says, "And what's your name?" The man
says, "Bella Paskin."

Sternberger says, "Mr. Paskin, please get off at the next station with me. I want to make a phone call for you." He didn't tell him anything. So, they get off and they go to a telephone booth and he tells the man to stay outside and he dials the number and after many rings, this woman picks up. He says, "Who am I speaking to?" And she says, "Maria Paskin."

And he says, "Maria, do you remember me? My name is Marcel Sternberger." She says, "Yes, I remember you." He says, "Maria, what was your husband's name?" She said, "My husband's name was Bella Paskin." He said, "Maria? You're about to witness the greatest miracle of your life. Hold on." And Bella Paskin comes in and Marcel hands the receiver to him. And Bella Paskin says, "Hello" to his long lost wife and she to her long lost husband. Separated by this world. Brought together by a simple miracle.

The final part of this story is that Marcel is standing outside the phone booth and he sees the man slap his forehead and screaming out of control with absolute disbelief. Not believing what had really happened. So Marcel is walking out with tears in his eyes and just thinking how this all happened.

He said, "You know what? I don't take this train. I don't live here. How did all this happen?" In the end, he gave the man some money to go and meet up with Maria, his wife, and he ends the article with this, the man writing the article says this, "Skeptical persons would no doubt attribute the events of that memorable afternoon to mere chance."

But was it chance that made Sternberger suddenly decide to visit his sick friend and take a subway line that he'd never been on before? Was it chance that caused the man sitting by the door of the car to rush out just as Sternberger came in? Was it chance that caused Bella Paskin to be sitting beside Sternberger reading a Hungarian newspaper? Was it chance or did God ride the Brooklyn subway that afternoon? You think you're here by accident? You think chance overrules God's destiny?

****

Every day, miracles happen all around you. Every day, God is at work in our world and our very own lives to show us that He is with us each and every day. Every day, angels are sent to us, many times without our even being aware of them, sent to us to help us to make decisions, make us smile for our neighbor, make us pick up that phone to invite someone over to be a part of our own world, make us see that, despite all that's going on, we're not alone.

Now, I don't believe in chances. I believe that whether I understand it or not, God has a hand in all of this. I'm just not able to understand it yet or even to comprehend it. I'd hate to have been one of the guys spoken to by God that are listed in our bible. Even the small amount that I've heard, I hesitate to tell a lot of people because they just think you're crazy or they try to write it off as something else.

And it's that way with being the disciple we were created to be. Talking to someone. Listening to them. Walking with them. They may not respond as you wish they would but what if it took three or four people before that person got it and you were not one of those three or four? What if something happened to them and they only heard one or two people spreading the words they needed to hear?

You know, God wouldn't have forced Mary to go through with what He chose for her to do. God didn't force Adam and Eve to not eat of the forbidden fruit. But, to show, to prove, to Mary that He was truly the one speaking through Gabriel, Gabriel told her about Elizabeth. Information that couldn't have been known since Elizabeth was sequestered away. Only those directly involved with the birth of John had insider knowledge.

But, we do put our trust out there too at times. There will be many that'll celebrate Christmas in the spirit that it was designed to be. A spirit of looking at what we have and giving thanks. A spirit of looking at who we can call our family and giving thanks. A spirit of trust that Christ really is the Savior and just going with that and giving thanks. Trusting that everything written in our bible is the whole truth and nothing but the truth.

But some would rather put their trust in just what they can feel, see and hear of this world. They have a sense that there's more but they just can't let go of what they can hold on to long enough to let that belief begin to breathe within them. Some have turned away from that promise of God of His Son because of something that has happened in the past.

Folks, God choses the ordinary to do the extraordinary. His promise is a new beginning for the ordering of the disorder in all of us and everything else around us. He uses ordinary people to achieve great things. He arms each of us with the truth that really does rule the day because the truth of what we do in the light of His grace will always outshine the darkness that the lies of this world tries to convince us of.

The story illustrates that you and me are the angels sent by God to deliver the Good News. We're tasked with it regardless if we're aware of it or not. We're designed with this task in mind whether we're comfortable with it or not. We've been given a blessing in being able to be the messengers of God even if we're afraid. God gives us the courage to take actions.

So it would seem to the man in the story. Imagine if he hadn't done what he did. Imagine if you miss the chance too.

<u>SIGNS</u>

What's Really Yours and What Belongs to God?

Gospel – Matthew 21:33 – 46

References – Psalm 118:22 – 23; Isaiah 5:1 – 7

There once was a couple that had inherited a piece of property. Now this property consisted of several plots and it was ideally situated on the shore of a very large lake. A big problem was that the couple didn't live on that property themselves and could only come to visit it about every other year. The property also had a neighbor which was seldom seen.

On one such visit, as the couple were boating by the property, they noticed that a fence the neighbor had erected seemed to be a little over their property line but they didn't give it much thought. A couple of years later, the couple again boated by and noticed that the fence line had moved a little and now there was also trash just on the other side of it, on their property. Again, the couple didn't give it much thought.

As one would have it, they again were boating by a couple of years later and they noticed the fence had really moved much farther into their property and a small barn was built on it.

This time, the couple confronted the neighbor who he told them that possession is 9/10s of the law and to take him to court.

The couple found, through the courts, that their neighbor now had imminent domain over their property because it was considered abandoned since no improvements had been made to it. Thus, the couple were thrown out of their inheritance.

****

Two thousand plus years ago, it was the law of the land, in Israel, that possession was, or could be, determined by occupancy. Since the people of that day were, somewhat, hostile to the land owners, they welcomed this law.

But the taking of property by any means, that were flagrantly unlawful, didn't convey the property over to those who committed those acts according to the laws of the time which were governed by Leviticus.

Hence, Jesus was using this parable to have the rulers of His day take a look at their own shortcomings and actions that stood in the same vein as the vine-growers. Jesus was using this parable of the wicked tenants as an illustration that would show the rulers of His day that the many rules and regulations they produced in that day were at odds with the real laws that they were based on. The laws of God given to Moses.

Jesus was using this parable to show that the rulers of His day were using the very fear committed by the vine-growers against the landowner then as we also see in our own nation today.

The wall written about, here, is synonymous with the laws enacted to separate the Jews from the Gentiles. The twelve tribes of Israel were planted in this vineyard that was surrounded by the wall of God's laws. The very geographical location of Palestine aided in this separation because of the high Lebanon Mountains on the north and the Mediterranean Sea on the west.

The wine press is the laws of Moses that were supposed to keep everyone on the straight and narrow.

The stone that Jesus spoke about was the very stone used as the basis of God's creation of Israel but it could also be the one used as a millstone to deny acceptance into the kingdom of God to those who see the creation by God as their own ownership rather than that of God. Those who rejected this very foundational stone of God.

Jesus is telling this story to have the rulers of His time look at the short history of the people and get it into their heads that all the minutia of laws they have created puts them at odds with the simple ten that were handed down by God to Moses.

They did this to claim ownership of the people they deemed not worthy to sit at their table because this lure of power was just too great. Claim ownership of the very faith of the people they were supposed to be the vine-growers to.

Much of the time, though, our own view is actually ruled by fear. The fear of what someone else might have. The fear of what someone else might earn. The fear of what someone else might take and the fear of the fear that gets created when we're informed by the Pharisees of our day.

The vineyard that Jesus was speaking about evokes the vineyard spoken about in our Isaiah 5:1-7 verses. It shows the vineyard to really be the sole possession of God, Himself. That all we are is caretakers of that vineyard. How we treat those that abide within that vineyard.

And that's where the problem resides. And that's where your fear is placed. Because, folks, if you put yourself above God then you'll eventually fear God and then you'll begin to fear what comes next. What happens to my life after it's gone.

Folks, I believe this Gospel is calling all of us to reexamine the value we place on our neighbor because we're the vine-growers in the parable being met each and every day by the slaves, the prophets and the word, sent by the landowner, God and Jesus, to collect the fruits, those we are supposed to have witnessed to, of the vineyard.

The parable illustrates that we can float by and be an onlooker, only to lose all that we cared about because we haven't tended to the land, or the vineyard, or we can become involved in the lives of those we're called to do and produce good fruit in them that will last from that vineyard.

TRUTH

Location, Location, Location

Gospel – Matthew 16:13 – 20

References – Isaiah 51:1; Acts 19; Galatians 2

Recently, there was a small community in Florida in the news. The homes and land were sinking due to unknown caves underneath. Another, near Austin, Texas, began sinking because of other caves that had been explored as far back as the early 1800s. Recent explorers found an old car trapped there.

Every now and then, we hear of such things. These communities begin to sink because their deeper foundations, foundations created by God, are either ignored or are unseen or because what we want is put at a higher priority than those of God. We think we know better than God.

So, every now and again, God reminds us that what He creates, or has created, cannot be ignored indefinitely. So it goes with us and our relationship with the Creator of all things. We wish our will over the will of God.

And the end result is that our own version of our realities begins to sink and crater with the reality of the truth. The caves are but an illustration of who's really in charge after all.

****

Location, location, location. Isn't that what people say when they look for prime real estate to buy? Location. Our Gospel, today, also has everything to do with location and the illustration that what God has created doesn't always fit with what we've come up with.

Sometimes, we can be in a place that we just wonder what happen. Either physically or mentally we probably all have experienced that at some point in our lives. The disciples were no different. They followed Jesus all over the place and would continue to follow His instructions until their own journeys would be cut short.

This Gospel starts out by giving the location where Jesus assigns His rock. The rock of the church. The Petra. Simon Peter. Both Matthew and Mark lists Caesarea Philippi as the starting place for this new church. The new body of believers. The new Ecclesia.

Caesarea Philippi is about 20 miles north of the Sea of Galilee. It was the site of a Baal cultic center. Baal was a fertility god and was considered central in that region. During the Hellenistic times, Baal became known as Paneas, the God of Pan, who was the one they worshipped to increase their flocks and increase the return on their fields. This god is sometimes shown as a goat that sits around and plays the flute.

However, this area was overtaken by Rome and renamed by Herod, the Great, after which he built a temple to Caesar Augustus. After the death of Herod, it was made a part of the territory owned by his son, Philip. Philip renamed it after Tiberius Caesar and himself and so, it was called Caesarea Philippi.

The point of all of this is that Jesus could have chosen any spot to ask His disciples the big question, "Who do people say that the Son of Man is?" He could've chosen on the shores of the Galilee right after He fed the 5000 and then 4000 people. He could've chosen just about any place else. But He chose the shadows of Caesar's temple.

And the confession of Simon. As the spokesperson for the other disciples acknowledged the discovery that, in front of the history and majesty that must've been Caesar's temple, the one who rose above it all, rose above even Caesar's temple, was Jesus. The Son of the living God.

You see, when Simon spoke out above the other disciples, he wasn't speaking for just him alone. He was speaking for all the disciple then and he speaks for us here and now. Simon, now Peter, represents the Christian faith in general. He represents you and me. But Peter is the foundation, not the builder. That's left up to you and me just as it was up to the disciples of Jesus' time.

As the rock, Peter was the person to which one could go to for information and revelation as to what God and Jesus are speaking about. The one with eyes to see and ears to hear. As the holder of the keys he is to be the teacher, not the one that's the holder to the gates of Heaven or Hell because, as we all should know, only God has that authority.

But if church leaders water down what's in this Gospel in order to appease the masses or to go along to get along or to relativize the very real words and meaning to follow the current trends, make everyone feel good, prosperity Gospel, then they'll be like the houses that were built above the caves and will sink and disappear because they're really built and exist only on shifting sand, broken stone, and mud.

The parable illustrates that what we base our belief on or in will cause us to react to different things differently. It also determines where we will end up in eternity. Once we accept that God really is the one in charge, then the belief we have on our faith can begin to blossom and develop firm foundations. Without that belief in God, we are on shaky grounds because we're determining ourselves to be God and we are broken.

TRUTH

Remember Change

Gospel – Mark 8:27 – 9:1

References – Proverbs 2:8; Matthew 16:22; 2nd

Corinthians 4

Years ago, people used to walk from one place to another. Then came the horse. Then came the car and roads and bridges. Then came the airplane. And with that the time that it took to go from the west coast to the east coast was reduced to hours rather than the years it took to walk it or even ride a horse. Along with those changes came distance.

Distance between people because one could get in the car or the plane and be at work in a matter of hours. No longer were people stuck with working in the town factory or store, they could branch out. The suburbs came into being and distance became greater. The distance between people.

Now, we have the internet where we can work from home. Be at work with the click of a button but the distance, the distance of people, got larger and more impersonal. But people have learned to overcome that distance.

More and more people gather together in smaller groups. Trying to maintain that closeness. Maintain that personal connection. Where people, in the days when you would have to walk, said goodbye to their families forever if they were moving across state lines to saying goodbye until the next holiday or family get together.

Change has happened and, in some instances, it has made things worse because it has created a distance between people so that interpersonal relationships become faint. In others, it has made people more direct in their attempts at maintaining what relationships they have. Change.

Change is something that cannot be stopped. Jesus is saying what are you gonna do with the change that is impending. Jesus is saying that your change of place should not change your place in the changes that are on your horizons.

****

Change. The world we face is ever changing. It's something that we all face day to day but, for the most part, we ignore it until we're slapped in the face with it. From changes that we encounter in our personal lives, our health, our families, or our surrounding societies to changes that happen that are beyond our control. Change is something that we just can't get away from nor is it something that we should shy away from either.

Jesus spoke about change a lot. Change from the way that we deal with others, our neighbors, to change in the way that we view our relationship with the one true God. Jesus says that change is probably the only secular thing we can count on. But what we can always count on to never change is our relationship that God has with us.

The more things change the more they stay the same. We all shy away from newness. Sometimes, though, we're pressed hard and can no longer ignore it. This change. But we tend to hold onto those things which have become comfortable. We like the things to be the way they were in the good old days. We like to hold onto those old ideas and memories because they're what we can count on. They're safe and a bit less fearful. A bit more secure.

Jesus says that the uncomfortable path, the road that's filled with potholes and cliffs is the road that we must follow. "Let them deny themselves and take up their cross and follow me. For those who want to save their life will lose it" is an invitation to follow the one that gives final rest to our own weary souls and rids our suspicions of all that's different.

It's said that there are only three things, three life moments, that change a person's inner core. A life or death occurrence, a severe change in life circumstances, and/or a religious experience. Everything that we hold dear will generally fall into one or more of those three events. Now, Jesus is saying that avoiding these events doesn't alter what will happen – just who you'll end up being after they occur.

But change, the kind of change Jesus is speaking and preaching about allows others to be members of the body of Christ, the family of God. But we want to remain safe. It's natural because the world is just not a safe place. With all that's going on, we do good to just wake up each day and live through another without harm.

So, you know what? God's telling us to remember the change and safety of His hands that has occurred in the past is here in our present. That we can be safe in His family. That we should all remember what Christ did for us on the cross and the sacrifice of God's only Son for the safety and change of you and me.

The parable is really an illustrations of how people use the change in their lives to either promote their relationships with others or enhance them. With the ability of the times to connect people, the barriers to keeping those connections get smaller and smaller. The change is your gauge to determine if you will stay connected to the people that you love. The traveling advances in the parable is to illustrate that worldly obstacles are not the real obstacle to connections to people. Your own created obstacles are those imagined barriers to connections to those you know and love.

<u>TRUTH</u>

To Divide Does Not Conquer

Gospel – Matthew 22:15 – 22

One day, a long time ago, there were two churches in a mid-sized town. Each had a large following but each had a very different way of looking at what was going on in the world around them.

The first church I'll call "The Statics". They looked at the world through very static lens and were able to find scripture that bore their way of thinking out and the ultimate mission of God on this earth.

The second church I'll call "The Depends". Everything, to them, depended on the state of human affairs but they also were able to use scripture to support their view of the world around them and the interaction between humans and God.

"The Statics" and "The Depends" fought with each other and, soon enough, wouldn't even speak to each other. They would quote passage after passage to enshrine what they truly believed not only in their church doctrine but also in the minds of their followers. This led to an even wider schism that soon enveloped the whole of the country side.

Finally, one day, a visitor was invited to the town to decide who was right. He listened with intent to each trying to sell their own point of view. After several weeks, the visitor then had all the people gather in the town square where he told them that while each side had very valid points, were ardent believers, followed their view of faith sincerely, what they missed in all their posturing was the fact that Christ came to change the normal course of events using the static laws handed down by Moses while allowing for current trends to base themselves on those static laws and, at the same time, bring a newer understanding of what His message was really all about.

Christ actually said yes to both and no to division.

****

The poll tax, referenced here, was a census tax established in 6 CE. Since this tax could only be paid in Roman coinage and the image on that coin was Tiberius Caesar, the general feeling of the Jews, of that day, was that even holding this coin was tantamount to agreeing with the edicts of that hated ruler.

The Jews, then, looked at this coin as a way to always remind them of the station they were in. Nothing like the glory days of old. They schemed and schemed and certain groups emerged because the Jews just couldn't operate unless they had a structure telling them what to do.

The Pharisees and the Herodians, mentioned here, hated each other with a vengeance. The Pharisees are represented, in our parable this morning, as "The Statics" and the Herodians are "The Depends". The Herodians were aligned with Herod, hence the name. These two disparate groups came together to entrap Jesus in answering a no win question.

But Jesus turned it around. He answered in a way that showed dividing does not, indeed, conquer. If Jesus had answered the Pharisees and the Herodians with an answer of no, then the Roman authorities would have labeled Him to be a rebel and He could've been crucified because of that charge. If Jesus had answered their question with a yes, then those same Pharisees and Herodians would have taken His answer to be against the very Jewish people themselves.

Any way that Jesus would answer would give ammo to those who were bent on persecuting Him and getting Him out of the way. Much like we see today. People on one side seeking to eliminate those on the other. This attitude has been used so much that a whole cancel culture has been born.

The movement has grown exponentially over the years as those students in these institutions of higher learning have graduated and actually learned to not learn. In other words, disagreement increases knowledge because adults are supposed to go and look at why they have a stance, or a belief, or an opinion, and cement or change or even rationally support that view.

But, the culture that has fermented for well over 20 years has grown to the point that even close relatives have distanced themselves with anger over things that have nothing to do with their own reality and over things which are so far out of their everyday lives and relationships.

The cancel culture is alive and well today in destroying structures by preying on our most basic of instincts – fear. But this culture, which we see even in our area because it's everywhere, is really only supported by fact less opinion.

So it is with Jesus and the Pharisees and the Herodians. Jesus with those He was trying to get to see the bigger picture and, thereby, help them to see that the truth is irrelevant of baseless opinion because God's truth overshadows all of the world's truth, and the Pharisees with those they were trying to lord over so that they could secure and keep their own worldly power.

Each sought to divide and thereby conquer those persons they saw as their subjects. Each side using their position to claim victory through the others defeat. Each trying to claim lordship over the other through each side's legalese and each side's humanism. Humanism is defined as the human condition being supreme over the divine. In other words, relativism.

But Jesus was the one that said, "Wait a minute." The issue is not division but unification. The bigger picture. The issue is not the physical abstract law or even the human condition but about what do you do in serving God that defines those very boundaries.

The real coin is not the one with Caesars image printed by humans on it but the coins with the image of God. That image of the creator that we have imprinted our own hearts. What He said, in effect, was that the two kingdoms, Heaven and earth are to be taken together as a whole. Not divided into one or the other.

So, the question today is, what do you see as your bias. Your way of approaching this Jesus and God and heaven and earth thing. Which side of the coin do you end up on when it's flipped in the forever throne room of God?

So it is regarding what you hold dear. It can warm the souls of all the others you come into contact with by you and me being the disciples we already are or, you and me can go home and contemplate and never tell another soul in which case only we will be warmed by those assuring words handed down in this bible. In either case, the rest of the world is getting colder and colder.

This parable illustrates how we can move to one side of the human equation and get stuck there because of our pride and our desire to be right. What we miss is the grace and mercy that comes from incorporating both sides into the same equation – our lives. Jesus answers a no win question. In do so, He shows that both side of humanity must be seen and followed because everyone and no one is humanly stuck in that rut.

TRUTH

Uncomfortable Cross

Gospel – Mark 8:31 – 9:1

References – 1st Corinthians 13

There once was a man who was true to his word but lived a very contradicted life. He would walk around town all the while aiming straight for his destination. He hurried everywhere he went only to have to wait for the other party to show up. His work was considered essential by most in the town but was sometimes put on hold if another emergency came up.

He was an early user of Microsoft Works, the word processor, but it always seemed to be broke. He graduated from college with an advanced degree in banking but seemed to have very little common sense. He lived in a very large house but had a relatively small family.

He saved most of his money but only by spending all of his time shopping for the best bargains. He considered the opinion of most others he heard but his own viewpoint was very narrow. He always seemed to be doing things to fill his life with projects but he was always involved with his work so his own life seemed to be empty.

He learned how to make a living, just not a life. He said he was filled with enough faith to move a mountain but never seemed to move another person to begin believing because this man was a Sunday only observer.

****

"For whoever wishes to save his life shall lose it; but whoever loses his life for My sake and the Gospel's shall save it." Paradoxical isn't it? I just listed, in our parable this morning, twelve paradoxes that I would bet could fit into any one of our lives. Maybe at least one or two?

A paradox is a statement or group of sentences that contradict what we know while delivering an inherent truth where as an oxymoron is a combination of two words that contradict each other. It's a dramatic figure of speech like clearly confused, jumbo shrimp, or bittersweet. Jesus is giving us a bit of both.

According to Jesus, in this Gospel, on the one hand if we wish to save our lives then we will lose our lives and, on the other, if we lose our lives for His sake, then we'll save our lives. Paradoxical and oxymoronic at the same time. We sometimes flock to hear about these abstract evils in the world and in the works of man but then we start hearing about things that pertain to our own eternal souls and the things that tug at our own eternal hearts and we just shy away.

But, Jesus is calling us to do just that. He says take up our crosses and follow Him. That following verse, the losing or saving of our lives, is defining what taking up our crosses really means. It means to abandon all our own thoughts about what we're supposed to do and simply follow Jesus wherever He leads us.

Taking up our cross is our giving up on what this world tells you is being a success and being satisfied that what God made you is and will be truly the finest. Taking up our cross is our act that realigns our way of thinking to match that which God has already laid out for us.

But being this cross bearer is paradoxical to our core emotions. Our core intuition that tells us that to be someone, we gotta be the best and get to the top. The problem, folks, is that those measurements are human constructs. They are measurements that pit one person against another.

I believe that we can reflect on where we are and prepare for where we can go. Where we can show up. I believe that we can overcome the fears put on us through this world and move forward with concentrating on the power of the cross which will allow us to put that fear on the back burner.

We turn away from truth because it's inconvenient and not in keeping with what we want to hear. We turn away from the cross itself because someone, somewhere, said we're following something that can't be verified.

The parable illustrates that our lives are a constant mix of signals and emotions and the conflict in each of us is what do we put our trust in. We attempt to follow the truth but that same truth is sometimes nuanced so much that it becomes a muddle mass of contradictions and then we're left wonder what went wrong. This parable shows that we live with that challenge each and every day and we're tasked with reading through the compost of words in this life to see the truth of God so we can be with Him in the next life.

APPENDIX

Parable	Verses	Subject
The Lost Seeking the Found	Matthew 2:1-12	Visit of the Wise Men
What is Your True Depth?	Matthew 4:23-25	Jesus Ministers to Crowds of People
	Matthew 5:1-12	Beatitudes
Inside vs. Outward Knowledge	Matthew 6:1-6	Concerning Almsgiving
	Matthew 6:16-18	Concerning Fasting
	Matthew 6:19-21	Concerning Treasures
Persistent Faith	Matthew 15:10-20	Things That Defile
	Matthew 15:21-28	Canaanite Woman's Faith
Location, Location, Location	Matthew 16:13-20	Peter's Declaration about Jesus
Our Stones that Cause Us to Stumble	Matthew 16:21-23	Jesus Foretells His Death and Resurrection
	Matthew 16:24-28	Cross and Self-Denial
Systemic Humanism and Humanity	Matthew 18:15-20	Reproving Another Who Sins
Shortchanging Forgiveness	Matthew 18:21-22	Forgiveness
	Matthew 18:23-35	Parable of the Unforgiving Servant
What is My End Motivation?	Matthew 20:1-16	Parable of the Laborers in the Vineyard
What Do You Really	Matthew	Authority of Jesus Questioned

	21:23-27	
Want to Know?	Matthew 21:28-32	Parable of the Two Sons
What's Really Yours and What Belongs to God?	Matthew 21:33-46	Parable of the Wicked Tenants
Where Is The Party?	Matthew 22:1-14	Parable of the Wedding Banquet
To Divide Does Not Conquer	Matthew 22:15-22	Question about Paying Taxes
Is Our Oil for Our House or Our Heart?	Matthew 25:1-13	Parable of the Ten Bridesmaids
So – What Have You Done Lately?	Matthew 25:14-30	Parable of the Talents
Our Ethics in the Light of God	Matthew 25:31-46	Judgment of the Nations
Have the Trumpets Blown?	Mark 1:1-8	Proclamation of John the Baptist
Just Do It	Mark 1:1-8	Proclamation of John the Baptist
	Mark 1:9-11	Baptism of Jesus
	Mark 1:12-13	Temptation of Jesus
	Mark 1:14-15	Beginning of the Galilean Ministry
Ordinary to The Extraordinary	Mark 1:9-11	Baptism of Jesus
	Mark 1:12-13	Temptation of Jesus
	Mark 1:14-15	Beginning of the Galilean Ministry
	Mark 1:16-20	Jesus Calls the First Disciple
On First Blush	Mark 1:21-28	Man with an Unclean Spirit
Status Quo Rebellion	Mark 1:29-34	Jesus Heals Mary at Simon's House

Made in the USA
Monee, IL
12 July 2021

72723651R00144